The Last Bus:
Time Matters

Dr. Deborah E. Kuhns
Dr. Gregory M. Kuhns

ISBN:1477468137
ISBN-13: 978-1477468135

DEDICATION

To our families with love. They have blessed us with the
joy we need to feel creative.

ACKNOWLEDGMENTS

We wish to thank all those family members and colleagues who have read our book to provide us with opinions, suggestions, and corrections.

CHARACTERS

Students

- ❖ Sarah – peacemaker; 7th-grade
- ❖ Jacob – robotics competition; 8th-grade
- ❖ Celeste – a thinker; 8th-grade
- ❖ Jessica – organized and meticulous; 8th-grade
- ❖ Max – board member's son; 6th-grade
- ❖ Alexandria – quiet; 5th-grade
- ❖ Carlyle – spelling bee winner; 7th-grade
- ❖ Melanie – keeps everyone happy and a cheerleader; 8th-grade
- ❖ Stan – holds his own and makes quick decisions; 8th-grade
- ❖ Nadialee – pulls people together for a cause; 7th-grade
- ❖ Ryan – led prayers at lunch; 7th-grade
- ❖ Austin – 7th-grade
- ❖ Benjamin – 5th-grade
- ❖ McKenzie – 6th-grade
- ❖ Caitlin – 5th-grade
- ❖ Zackary – 8th-grade
- ❖ Cameron – 5th-grade
- ❖ Lauren – 6th-grade
- ❖ Julianna – 7th-grade
- ❖ Darius – 6th-grade

Adults

- ❖ Mark Rollins – Principal
- ❖ Mrs. Williams – teacher
- ❖ Miss Johnson – school secretary
- ❖ Danny – custodian
- ❖ Transportation Director
- ❖ Miss Stern – skills' teacher
- ❖ Raole – man with the duffle bag
- ❖ Harman C. Bernard – Superintendent
- ❖ John Sterling – Board member
- ❖ David Warren – school bus driver
- ❖ Stewart – replaced school bus driver
- ❖ Jo Lee – added to bus when it stopped
- ❖ Marta – added to bus when it stopped
- ❖ Liz Rollins – wife of Mark Rollins
- ❖ Board President
- ❖ Sargent Denise Fazio – police woman
- ❖ Captain Duncan – police officer

CHAPTER 1

The call came in at nine o'clock in the morning as the bell was ringing for second period at North Middle School. That's how the principal, Mr. Mark Rollins, recalled later the exact time that he received the phone call and heard the demand, "Get a school bus and put twenty students on it by ten o'clock or your entire school will be blown up. I'll call back at one minute till ten. Don't think I'm kidding. And don't talk about this with anyone, or none of you will see tomorrow." Then a click and he was gone.

Was this a joke? What had just happened? Now what? With all these fragmented thoughts running through his head, Mr. Rollins began to react. He couldn't take a chance on it possibly being a prank. At ten o'clock it would be too late to wonder. With shaking hands he ran his fingers through his thinning hair and reached for the class rosters. He reasoned that his first priority was keeping the majority of students safe. He remembered later that he truly believed in those first few moments that even if twenty students did get taken away, they would surely be set free later.

Where to begin now – by grade level, ten girls and ten boys, or randomly? Nothing had ever prepared him for this. When he came to work this morning the only dilemma he had envisioned was whether he could get a fire drill in before it rained. Now he was faced with life and death decisions, and he felt like his head was splitting. The usual serenity within this office and in Mr. Rollins was rattled.

If twenty honor roll students were selected, they might be able to plan an escape from their captors. On the other hand, if the students were never to return, the loss of twenty of the brightest would greatly affect the town's genetics for generations. Furthermore, could twenty gifted and talented students work together to plot a solution for escape? That was highly unlikely given the confusion at the last student council meeting when planning the homecoming dance. Now choosing a DJ that appealed to four grades of middle school students seemed insignificant compared to choosing twenty students who might never be seen again.

Minutes were ticking by. Irrelevant thoughts seemed to pass through his consciousness. Concentrating seemed impossible. His wife kept telling him to drink less caffeine. Maybe after this he would consider taking her advice.

A teacher came to the office door to ask about the spirit assembly planned for next week. He could count on Mrs. Williams to be conscientious and plan ahead. His secretary said he had a phone call from a parent. He asked her to take a message for now. The shuffle of the custodian's feet coming toward the office undoubtedly meant that he wondered when he planned to have the fire drill. "Hey, Danny, let's skip that fire drill today. Tomorrow's weather is calling for sunshine." The custodian seemed to derive a lot of pleasure from getting to ring the fire alarm. He looked mildly disappointed about having to wait until the next day.

Mr. Rollins tried to focus. Maybe closing the door might help. He needed to call the transportation director to get a bus brought to the school. Maybe he won't ask too many questions about North Middle School suddenly planning a trip. That was probably too much to hope for since the buses were extremely well-protected as if they were personally owned by the director of transportation instead of the school system.

His thoughts continued to selecting students. Sarah. Pick Sarah. She's a peacemaker. Jacob did well in the robotics competition. Shawn – not Shawn. He gets angry too easily. Celeste is a thinker. Jessica is organized and meticulous. Too many girls. He needed more boys. Too many 8th-graders. There needs to be a few younger students. Max is the son of a School Board member. Pick him. Don't pick him. When it is discovered that Mark alone chose twenty students to be led into certain death, what would he face? He needed to not think of that now. There will be time to dwell on his poor judgment later.

Now the digital clock read 9:33 a.m. He had wasted more than half the time given to him not being able to focus. He still needed to hear back from transportation.

Yes, take Max. He'll need the board member to care about getting the students returned. That's five. Another girl. Find a 5th-grader. One who's quiet? Alexandria. How about Carlyle? He's the 7th-grade spelling bee winner. Melanie will keep everyone happy. She's a cheerleader. Stan will hold his own and make quick decisions.

No, he couldn't tell the transportation director now on the phone where the bus would be going. Even if he knew, he couldn't tell him. Just believe that it's important. Okay, the bus was on its way. It was now nine forty. Twelve students to go. Nadialee knew how to pull people together for a cause. Ryan leads prayers at lunch. That would be needed. Half-way there. Don't analyze. Just pick ten more names, get the twenty students, and put them on the bus. A perfect solution – just go to the nearest class and take ten students into the hallway. As he walked through the office again running his fingers through what hair he had left, he told his secretary to call the ten students he had chosen to come to the office. It is always peculiar how at truly odd times an unrelated thought pierces your thought pattern and interrupts what needs to be accomplished. Like now, when he thought of his wife again, who has cautioned him many times that running his fingers through his hair just might be causing his hair to get thinner.

He kept moving through the office and on down the hall. Skills class. That's where he could find ten more students from all different grades. His rubber-soled shoes could be heard squeaking down the hall as he hurried to room 413 and told Miss Stern that he needed ten students to come with him. As he waited in the hallway he had a fleeting doubt about his compliance with the caller's demand. Maybe he should wait to see what would happen if he didn't produce a bus and twenty students. But as often happens in life, we just do the next thing even as we question the wisdom of our action. The students came out of Miss Stern's class and he told them to go to the office. It was as simple as that. The students in this school rarely questioned authority. They walked quietly on the right side of the hall, keeping their hands to themselves, just as they had been taught. On his way back up the hall Mr. Rollins walked ahead of the students and saw that the bus was pulling up in front of the school. The transportation director had come through after all.

Count heads. There's twenty. "Students, there's a bus out front. Please quietly go get on it." Wait. He needed to know the names of all the students who would be leaving. "Miss Johnson, please write the students' names on a list as they leave to get on the bus."

The phone was ringing. The digital clock said 9:58. Maybe it's not him. "North Middle School. This is Mr. Rollins."

"You follow directions well. I hope you chose wisely. Time will tell, but lives will soon depend on the choices you made. Now go outside beside the bus and I will call you on your cell phone."

Mark wondered how he knew his cell phone number. He felt the vibration in his pocket and knew that it didn't matter. He just needed to answer it.

Where was he calling him from? "Mark, surely you won't mind if I call you by your first name. Now comes the tough part. In just a minute a man named Raole is going to walk up and get on the bus. He'll be wearing a green ball cap and carrying a duffle bag. The doors will close and you will walk back into the school and go to your office. Do not say anything to anyone. Just go through the rest of your day. I'll be calling you."

As Mr. Rollins turned to walk away from the bus he heard students yelling out, "Mr. Rollins, where are we going? Why is there no teacher? When will we be back? How will our parents know when to pick us up? Mr. Rollins – Wait!" And then immediate silence as Mr. Rollins glanced back and saw the man in the hat stand up and face the children while reaching into his duffle bag.

CHAPTER 2

It was just the beginning. It wasn't even time for first lunch and he felt like he was emotionally drained. No one knew anything yet. Third period was just beginning and he could hear the intercom buzzing from several teachers asking Miss Johnson where some students were whose names had not been on the absence list. Her consistent response was, "I'll check." She knew they had boarded a bus while Mr. Rollins stood and watched, but she was too professional to ask him why. But how long could they keep pretending?

Miss Johnson knew by lunch there would be many questions that would soon need to be answered. She herself was curious, but the look on Mr. Rollins' face when he came back into the office from outside made her swallow hard and not ask. This was only her third year as his secretary, but she had learned that when he looked preoccupied with serious thoughts, it was not the time to ask questions. She was single and needed her paycheck. She could not afford to lose this job by questioning her boss.

The first call about the situation came from Mr. Bernard, the Superintendent of Schools, before it was time for the first lunch. Of course the transportation director had reported to him a spontaneous trip for twenty students with no authorization. Now the superintendent wanted an explanation from Mr. Rollins. "Can you tell me why twenty students have gone on a trip without a request and with no destination?"

Mr. Rollins responded, "No, I can't."

To which the superintendent responded, "You can't tell me that?!"

Again Mr. Rollins replied, "No, Mr. Bernard, I'm not able to tell you."

"I'm coming over there and we will get to the bottom of this."

Now a new dilemma. Mr. Rollins wondered if he should be open with the superintendent or give it some more thought until the first student didn't make it home after school. That was only hours away. Would a few more hours make a difference? It might if the caller contacted Mr. Rollins and told him what was happening. Meantime, Mr. Rollins wondered what to name him besides "caller." Should he refer to him as a kidnapper, a terrorist, a murderer, a schizophrenic?

It wasn't that long of a ride from the board office to the middle school. Within minutes the superintendent will be here asking questions and the transportation director will come along. He wondered where this conversation would go.

He didn't have long to wait. As he anticipated, both the superintendent and the transportation director arrived together to speak with him and sat in the two chairs facing his desk. Maybe telling them would help to relieve him of the sole responsibility of this overwhelming situation. That hope was short-lived as the superintendent listened to a brief description of the day's events before interrupting, "So, let me see if I have this straight. Some phone caller threatened to blow up the school with no evidence of that being true whatsoever and demanded twenty of our students and a bus, and you just gave it all to him?! At any time did you consider calling me to ask what to do or did you even for a brief moment think about calling the police or having the phone call traced or removing all the people from the school and evacuating to another location? Did you even think at all?!" His face was turning a deep red and his voice became a booming sound that filled the office.

This was not going well, but it was just as he predicted. He was wrong and nothing he had done was acceptable. "But he knew my cell phone number and my name."

"So does everyone who has access to our school directory on-line! Anyone in the country could know that information! I can't believe that with fifteen years of experience as a principal you just handed over – how many students? Twenty? At what point were you going to let someone know? Did it ever occur to you that this person may have just wanted a free bus and so now that he has what he wants he'll just eliminate the children? And while you weren't really thinking at all, did it seem possible that since we're the richest school system in the state this person may be going to hold our students for ransom? I can't even imagine what you were thinking!"

With a look of complete contempt toward Mr. Mark Rollins, he replied, "Let's quit discussing it and call the State Police, which is what you should have done hours ago." Mr. Rollins began to understand how students feel when they come to the principal's office.

Before he could reach for a phone, Mr. Rollins' cell phone rang. "So, Mark, who all have you told? I took you to be the kind of quiet person in charge who would just solve this problem all by yourself. Now, just to warn you, for every police car that shows up, a child will be lost. If you want that on your conscience, just keep talking."

Now faced with two opposing choices, Mr. Rollins looked at the superintendent and said, "I don't think we should call the police."

The superintendent said that it was not Mr. Rollins' choice to make and he would take care of it himself. Although Mr. Rollins explained what the caller had just told him, he was told by Mr. Bernard that he was no longer in charge. It was out of the principal's hands, as the call was made by the superintendent to the State Police.

That call set the activities in motion that basically left Mr. Mark Rollins out of the picture. In the midst of the phone calls to authorities and alerting the media, the transportation director was also chastised for not placing a tracking device in the bus before turning it over to the kidnapper.

CHAPTER 3

"An ongoing development involving twenty kidnapped students from a county outside of the nation's capital is now in the process. Apparently a school bus provided by the county itself drove away from North Middle School this morning at ten o'clock a.m. with the kidnapper aboard after the principal was contacted by an unknown caller who reportedly threatened to blow up the school if a bus and twenty students were not provided. A motive for this kidnapping has not been determined. We will follow this story as it develops. Attempts will be made to communicate with parents and board employees." Channel 12 news then went to another story.

The superintendent, Harman C. Bernard, had told Principal Mark Rollins that he was not to answer the phone or provide any information to anyone. He personally would take care of any communication. That didn't stop the phone calls that continuously came into North Middle. There was not enough of Miss Johnson to answer every call and there was not enough information to satisfy people. And what did the newscaster mean that the caller had *reportedly* threatened to blow up the school? *Reportedly!* Mr. Rollins paced as he wondered if they are now doubting that someone called him and saying that he might not have been threatened. That was absurd! Why would he make up a story like that and why would he endanger the lives of twenty children if he hadn't been threatened? Is it possible that the superintendent has started this doubt about his story? If they all can't trust each other, how were they going to be able to deal with a kidnapper or terrorist, or whatever he is? And we haven't even made it to the end of this school day when the other students at North Middle would be going home, he thought. But it won't be long.

Even as he began to plan how to deal with parents, Miss Johnson interrupted his thoughts.

"Mr. Rollins, John Sterling is on the phone and demands to speak with you. He's Max's father. He's also a board member. Did you remember that?"

"Yes, Miss Johnson, I know who John Sterling is. Please close my door on your way out."

Hello, Mr. Sterling. What can I do for you?" He had decided that remaining calm and answering questions directly would increase his credibility, which seemed to be in question.

"Mark, I will come right to the point. Why was my son, Max, put on a bus to an undisclosed destination with nineteen other students, and when did you plan to inform his mother and me and the other parents?"

"Mr. Sterling, I would like for you to help me. I don't know who has our twenty students, but in order to protect the remaining students from the threat of being blown up, I agreed to provide a bus that took our children somewhere. I don't apologize for my decision, but I think together you and I can find answers."

After a moment of silence in which Mr. Rollins braced himself for another tongue-lashing, Max's father said, "I appreciate your honesty. I'll do anything to get my son back."

Mr. Rollins let out the breath he had unknowingly been holding. He was relieved to finally have an ally.

Mr. Sterling and Mr. Rollins agreed to start by calling the parents and setting up a meeting at the school this evening. Although Mr. Bernard was communicating with the media, they decided that for this evening they would keep the media out of the meeting so that they could talk openly with parents who were obviously going to be upset.

Before hanging up the phone, Mr. Rollins provided ten of the names and phone numbers for Mr. Sterling so that they could begin to call parents to share the devastating news, and invite them to the school to discuss the events of the day and hopefully arrive at a solution to the dilemma.

CHAPTER 4

At a distant location, someone else was watching the news with interest and thinking, "No police cars so far, but it definitely has hit the news. It's only a matter of time, and then if the police get involved I will have to carry through with my threat – one kid for each police car. For now I will call the bus again to see where they are. I'm not quite sure about how well Raole can follow directions. The bus driver had seemed to understand where to drive, but Raole sure wouldn't know if they were in the right place."

It's about time, Raole thought, when he heard his cell phone ringing. "Yea, we're in Wild and Wonderful West Virginia. These kids want to eat and go to the bathroom, and I'm tired of being on this bus!"

After listening briefly into his phone, Raole said, "Yea, I have all their cell phones. How come kids all have cell phones now? We didn't even have a phone in our house until I was twelve."

Within the short conversation he had his next orders. Someday, he thought, I'm going to quit taking orders. After I get paid for this one, I'm doing what I want to do.

The bus began to slow down as it entered the town of LaVale, Maryland. For miles in the eastern panhandle of West Virginia the roads weave between states. Within the parking lot of the Days Inn Motel, the bus stopped long enough for some coolers and boxes to be loaded on the bus by two women and a man. Further instructions were given to the school bus driver as he was told to get off the bus while the new man, Stewart, took his place in the driver's seat.

Just that quickly the door closed and the bus moved on. The children groaned until one of the women spoke loudly and harshly, "That's enough!"

Raole looked at her and said, "Jo Lee – you don't have to yell at them. They've been good all day without me yelling at them."

Jo Lee's response was quick and nasty, "I'll do it my way! We're not being paid to be nice!" To which Marta, the other woman who had just entered the bus, replied, "It's always your way!" Jo Lee is a tall bleached-blond middle-aged woman who easily towered over Marta, a petite, but occasionally feisty, woman in her thirties.

Stewart, the man now driving the bus, said loudly, "Just once I'd like to drive in peace. The kids are quieter than you are!"

Raole spoke up next and said, "Speaking of the kids, they've been hungry for hours now and they need to use the bathroom. We need to stop."

After much discussion it was decided that they would go into the next rest stop with only a few of the students at a time using the restroom and getting a drink from the water fountain. No food for now. Jo Lee said that the children should feel grateful for water. Stewart and Jo Lee stood at the door of each restroom and allowed only one girl and one boy into the restroom areas at a time while monitoring the few in line, waiting to make sure there was no talking. The students were so fearful of their guards that for now they didn't attempt to communicate with each other. Alexandria stood with tears coming down her cheeks until she was yelled at by Jo Lee, which did not help Alexandria feel better. She turned her face away from Jo Lee to hide her tears and quivering chin.

Many of the students reluctantly boarded the bus again feeling hungry and worried and frustrated. They wondered what would happen to them next and where they were being taken.

CHAPTER 5

Channel 12 news was again reporting, "Now for further developments about the twenty kidnapped students in a school bus in the eastern part of the United States. The bus driver from the school system was let off the bus at a motel in LaVale, Maryland, within the last hour as an unknown man boarded the bus and got behind the wheel. Since his cell phone had been taken from him, the school system's bus driver, David Warren, then used the motel's phone to communicate with the superintendent.

"Mr. Warren reported that details of the destination were not discussed while he was on the bus. The kidnapper has not been identified. We are now receiving information that when the new bus driver got on the bus, apparently two females entered the bus with him before it took off again. Although

Mr. Warren can vaguely describe the assailants, the cameras for the Days Inn did not show any movements of the kidnappers since the bus was stopped in the back parking lot on the outer edge.

"The school system's bus driver has confirmed that the bus was travelling on Interstate 68 into West Virginia and that the kidnapper who originally boarded the bus at the school has a duffle bag that he said does have the explosives to be used if necessary. He also confirmed that the kidnapper agreed with someone who called him on his cell phone that no police cars have been seen, and that he understood that for each one that showed up a child would be eliminated.

"We will keep you posted on new developments, but for now Channel 12 News has been told that, although aware of the situation, the police are remaining at a safe distance to protect the children."

As the newscaster went on with other stories, the superintendent was heard to say in his office, "I don't care what the threat is, we have a board member's son on that bus and we need to get him off!"

CHAPTER 6

A few parents had not been reached, but as each one of their children did not arrive home, they called the school and the bus garage and the central board office. In each case they were given a brief explanation with what little information was available. Word spread about the parent meeting to be held at the school, including to the superintendent who had other plans and would not be attending. How would that look to the parents?

By quarter till seven the gymnasium was half full. By seven o'clock there was standing room only. This was obviously not just a parent meeting. This could easily become a lynch mob. This was not just a group of forty frantic parents. This was a group of hundreds of angry community members.

The first question set the tone for the evening.

"Why did we hear about this on national news before we knew anything about it here in our own town?"

"What's being done to get our children back?"

"Why did they pick this school?"

"Do you know where the kidnapper's from?"

"Why isn't the bus driver here for us to talk to?"

"When was the last time you heard from this terrorist?"

"Can we have the names of all the children?"

"What's the plan for getting the students back?"

"Have the kidnappers asked for money?"

"Do you personally know the kidnapper?"

"When are you supposed to hear from the kidnapper again?"

It went on for too long with growing frustration among the parents and increasing anxiety within Mr. Rollins as the questions continued with few available answers.

John Sterling finally contributed the voice of reason by telling the parents that the Board of Education had everything under control and would be keeping them informed. He added that they needed to listen to the superintendent and the principal, and not listen to rumors or misinformation. As Mr. Sterling and Mr. Rollins turned off the microphone and exited the gym, a father in the audience loudly said, "We'd like to listen to them, but they aren't telling us anything!" Parents began to hug each other and cry and express anger to anyone who was nearby.

Once in the hallway Mr. Sterling and Mr. Rollins walked quickly to the office where they closed and locked the door knowing they had no other information to offer the parents. It was now nine o'clock and the students had been gone for eleven hours. What he had read about the chance of survival of kidnapped children as time went by was a fleeting thought as Mark Rollins reached in his pocket for his cell phone that was vibrating. It was not a number he recognized as he answered it with a quick, "Hello."

The caller told him to not say anything – to just listen and be quiet. As the caller then continued with words he wasn't sure he wanted to hear, Mr. Rollins sat down and looked at Mr. Sterling with a forlorn expression.

"Listen carefully because this won't be repeated. Your students are being taken to another state. I suggest you call the media and tell them that you heard from me and that I'll be calling back some time with my list of demands. Don't hold your breath on when that might be. But meantime, the kids only stay alive as long as the police stay away. Be sure to tell them that."

And then the caller was gone, leaving Mr. Rollins sitting there in silence. Again he had the thought that no courses he took to become a principal had prepared him for any of this. He had a question of his own that he would like answered – why me and why our school?

CHAPTER 7

It was dark and the bus was finally slowing down. Some of the children were lying down on the seats asleep while others had their heads against the windows. When the bus came to a full stop they all began to wake up and listen to the adults talk.

It seemed again that Jo Lee was calling the shots. She told Raole to get off the bus and go unlock the door. From the bus the children could see a large dark house with no lights anywhere. The trees surrounding the house formed a fortress around it and stretched up into the gloom above it. After the door of the bus was opened they were told to go into the house and to be quiet with no talking. They were hanging onto each other as they blindly tripped in the dark over roots and rocks. Only a flash light held by Raole outside of the door of the house gave them an idea of where to walk.

When all of the children were inside the house, Raole lit a lantern to reveal a huge high-ceilinged room with old woodwork, windows covered with thick velvet curtains, and a large brick fireplace. As the children stood quietly watching, Marta and Jo Lee uncovered the aged furniture and threw the sheets layered with dust into the corner of the room. The Persian rugs and now exposed velvet Victorian furniture represented an era long past with a musty indescribable smell.

The room was so large that there were seats for them all, which they scrambled to sit on at the order of Jo Lee. The children had formed a tacit agreement among themselves that Jo Lee was not a person to reckon with. What she said they did, and the quicker the better to avoid her wrath.

A question was foremost in the children's thoughts, where were they and how would their parents find them? Second to that was a more immediate need about how they could get food. Without the question being asked, Marta offered, "How about I get the drinks and sandwiches out for the kids? They're probably starving. I know I am." And with that she opened coolers and boxes that had been stashed onto the bus during their brief stop to exchange bus drivers.

The children were not given choices, but all gratefully took a sandwich and drink when it was handed to them. As they sat quietly chewing and swallowing, their eyes roamed around the spacious room surrounding them. It felt like a museum with old paintings and decorations gracing the tops of tables and the mantle. With only one lantern on in the large room, the shadows cast by the furnishings and people led to a sense of being abandoned in a house long forgotten. The doors leading to the other rooms were open but the space was eerie and black. The spectacular long winding wooden staircase was barely visible in the darkness, but they imagined that it led upstairs to a second floor of more darkness and dust.

The adults said very little even when Stewart, who had been driving the bus, ventured off down the hallway with light from a flashlight that was soon swallowed up by the darkness. Although no one called out to him, the adults glanced at each other as he walked away. Was there meaning in their glances or were they just monitoring each other? The children sat quietly and speculated, but knew better than to ask. His disappearance for the moment caused them all to be grateful for each other's company. This realization would provide some comfort during the time ahead of them. But even the consolation brought by company and common situations can dissipate when survival becomes the priority. For now they weren't physically uncomfortable but without a doubt were emotionally distraught as they each began to envision their own families and the security of their own homes that seemed quite remote from where they were right now.

CHAPTER 8

Stewart had still not reappeared when Jo Lee announced that they would all be walking upstairs together to find rooms to sleep in. Even during these instructions, many of the children's eyes glanced toward the dark staircase and the blackness beyond. Their minds wandered and imagined what might exist there where their eyes could not penetrate the darkness. When Jo Lee finished telling them what they had to do, she commanded them to stand up and follow her as she headed toward the steps carrying the only lit lantern. That meant that those children toward the end of the line were scrambling to get ahead and not be left behind in the eeriness of the living room. Raole and Marta also seemed to walk briskly behind Jo Lee.

Although difficult to tell what was in each room, Jo Lee didn't seem to care as she opened doors and said at six different doors the names of the children who were to enter – three in some rooms and four in others. When designating who would go into a room, Jo Lee would briefly shine the lantern into it that allowed the children only seconds to hear their names and get into the room. They were then handed one small flashlight by Marta that would be shared among the occupants of each room.

Finally the twenty children were all divided up into bedrooms that were furnished with only beds and dressers. Once the children were all within their rooms, Jo Lee announced from the hallway that there was a bathroom at each end of the hall to be shared by all the children. At least there was indoor plumbing, because from what the children had seen of the old mansion they all had wondered where and when they would be able to use the restroom. At some point some owner had modernized the Civil War era house to bring it into the twentieth century to the relief of the children. Jo Lee determined which bathroom would be used by the girls and which one would be shared by the boys.

Within each bedroom, as with the rest of the house, the beds had sheets thrown over them to protect them from dust. Having observed as Jo Lee and Marta had removed the dust-covered sheets in the room below, the children all found themselves dutifully removing the sheets covering the beds before lying down and restlessly dozing while waiting their turns to use the restrooms. All were exhausted from their day's experience. A few anticipated what might be ahead for them. Others were beyond imagining and instead felt true fear.

Jo Lee had carefully divided the children based on some criteria known only to her, which had been determined in her mind based on which children would not get along with each other and would make each other's lives miserable. It was all a part of the way Jo Lee thought. Some people are only content if people around them are unhappy and in conflict with each other. Jo Lee was definitely one of those individuals who thrived on the misery of others. So, after analyzing the children while they rode on the bus and ate in the living room, she decided the groups would look like this: Room 1 – Sarah, McKenzie, Melanie; Room 2 – Jacob, Max, Carlyle; Room 3 – Celeste, Alexandria, Nadialee; Room 4 – Jessica, Caitlin, Lauren, Julianna; Room 5 – Stan, Ryan, Benjamin, Darius; Room 6 – Austin, Zackary, Cameron.

None were placed in a room with someone in the same grade. Jo Lee started realizing immediately how different 5th-graders were from 8th-graders, and could recognize how different each grade level of children acted. She had them write their names and grade levels down on a tablet she passed around as they rode on the bus. From that she had begun her division of children by combining different ages.

Next, she thought about the various ways the children handled the stress and how they reacted to each other. Some of the girls flirted openly with boys and some more quietly, while others ignored the boys altogether. She grasped quickly which girls seemed to be outgoing, and especially with boys, and which ones seemed to be content to quietly communicate with other girls or with no one at all. Jo Lee was perceptive, as well as deliberately vindictive. She wanted to prevent any meaningful interaction between the children as much as possible. It would be interesting to see how long that would be possible given the fact that the children were all in the same predicament. It's a well-known fact that sharing a fearful or unhappy situation can create a bond between people. There would be plenty of time to see if that happened with these children in their current circumstance.

CHAPTER 9

Austin was in the seventh grade and was somewhat of a loner. Most of the time, he did as he was told, but not every time. He did okay in school, but not all the time. People who knew him thought he was rather unpredictable. Some students feared him, while other students ignored him, and still others did not treat him kindly. Maybe it was that no one took the time to get to know him. On the other hand, those who thought they knew him well at times became aware of maybe why some students preferred not to be friends with him.

He was the one student that Jo Lee couldn't read or predict. Without a doubt, Jo Lee recognized that Austin was different. She knew he would have to be carefully watched because he had a look in his eyes that made her wonder what he was capable of. She remembered that look in the eyes of one of her former boyfriends who had ended up in prison. She and everyone else found out too late what he was capable of. Now she had doubts about Austin, which might also prove to be justified.

As the other nineteen children dozed, Austin stared up at the gray shadows on the ceiling above the beds. As his eyes adjusted to the dark, he could see Zackary and Cameron sleeping, and felt a mixture of emotions. Even while sleeping, Zackary looked like he thought he was just so cool and didn't have a care in the world. On the other hand, Cameron was curled in a fetal position, and while he slept he looked like he might cry at any minute. What a pair to be stuck with, Austin thought. One of them was lost in his own world of always trying to look cool and would never admit fear, and the other one was in his own world of missing mommy and daddy.

Austin had self-doubts on occasion, but he reasoned that staying away from others helped him to deal with it and to never show anyone that he was vulnerable. He realized that in his current situation the person he needed to pretend to get along with was Jo Lee. She was obviously in charge and definitely angry at the world. What happened in her life to make her so angry and miserable he could only imagine. Maybe kids picked on her when she was younger and she had suspected at a young age that if she acted tough they would be afraid of her and leave her alone. Even if it hadn't worked back then, she succeeded now in having people obey her. They might grumble behind her back, but to her face she was a force to be reckoned with, and nobody chose to do that. Austin was aware of all this, but decided that he was up for the challenge of playing mind games with Jo Lee to show her that not everyone was afraid of her.

And there was no time like the present to begin his mental assault on Jo Lee. So, while the other students slept, he used the small flashlight to explore. Austin decided that this whole game would be more fun if Jo Lee knew just enough to make her suspicious of everyone until he wanted her to suspect him. It wouldn't be fun at all if Jo Lee assumed that all the children were afraid of her. Austin wanted her to wonder who was causing problems before suspecting him, and then as time passed he wanted her to begin to fear him. That's the way he wanted to play this game. It would occupy him while they were stuck together in this abandoned mansion.

He wondered if, given enough time, he might get all nineteen students to comply with his demands as quickly as they did now with Jo Lee. That might be an even greater challenge, but he felt like he would soon be ready for that challenge also. It had been awhile since he truly tried to outsmart someone, but when he put his mind to something, there was no stopping him.

When he was in fifth grade, he had proven his intelligence when he was determined to win against all the older students at Academic Quiz Bowl. The teachers were astounded and the students congratulated him. But that was the beginning of middle school. Now they mostly stayed away from him. He had decided that other people congratulating him for being smart wasn't all that special anyway. He had tried sports last year in sixth grade and he was really good at cross country. He actually had found it invigorating to outrun other athletes effortlessly through the woods and even through creeks. But again, winning trophies didn't seem like a big enough challenge once he had achieved it. Now he was up for another challenge, and Jo Lee was it. She didn't know it yet, but she would soon.

Austin opened the door of the bedroom and walked toward the girls' bathroom. There was no one there. He went into the first room assigned to the girls that was closest to the bathroom. He remembered exactly who was in each room. He had paid very close attention as Jo Lee assigned rooms and, just in case he might forget, he saw Jo Lee throw down the list in the hallway and realizing how valuable that might be later, he had picked it up and stashed it in the pocket of his jeans. So, he knew that Melanie was in this room. And pretty blond that she was, when he opened their bedroom door just slightly he could see her light hair spread out over her pillow as she slept. He quietly approached her bed, thinking that even in her sleep she looked cheerful, and reached out and smoothed her hair and said, "Melanie," as he leaned close enough for his breath to touch her face. She woke up with a start, saw a shadow leaning over her, and began screaming.

Austin had been fully prepared for her reaction, and had been out the door and moving down the hall toward his own room before her first scream was finished. By the time the second scream started, he was in his own room with the door closed. By the time Sarah's and McKenzie's voices joined hers, he was in his own bed with the covers over him with his eyes closed, so that when Jo Lee, Marta, and Raole came around shining flashlights in everyone's faces to see if they were asleep, Austin could look the picture of innocence, while he thought, "Let the games begin."

On the eleven o'clock news that night across the nation the newscaster reported, "The whereabouts of the school bus with twenty middle-school students is unknown. The trail was lost somewhere in West Virginia. The mountains made it difficult for the police to follow at a safe distance. It's almost as though the bus with the children disappeared from the face of the earth. Hopefully this won't be the last bus that these students ride on. Our sympathy goes out to the parents and to the school."

CHAPTER 10

Far from the abandoned mansion, a cell phone was being used to call Jo Lee, who was still wide awake after trying to calm the girls. Melanie seemed almost distraught enough to be believed, but Jo Lee found no boys awake when she made her rounds. Maybe Melanie just had a nightmare.

"Hello. This is Jo Lee," was her response.

"Well, we need no introductions. You know who this is. I tried calling Stewart, but he didn't answer. I hope our remarkable bus driver has not met with any harm. When you see him, tell him that he'll get more than his share for losing the police. So far he seems to be the only one of you doing anything outstanding. Keep those kids under control and you might be lucky enough to get a bonus too. For now, no one seems to have any idea where the kids are hidden, so let's keep it that way. It may just take a long time to list our demands so that the school system will get desperate enough to give us anything we want."

Then he was gone. Jo Lee was left wondering herself what the demands were, because usually as long as she gets paid she just does the job without asking. But this time it seemed relevant and maybe more worth her while to know since they had actually kidnapped children, which she had never done before. Kidnapping children and stealing a school bus seemed like serious stuff that would lead to life in prison, and she sure didn't want to go there.

She also wondered why Stewart wasn't answering his cell phone, even when the big boss was calling him. That didn't make sense. Surely he didn't fall asleep and not hear his cell phone. That was one of the cardinal rules in their job description – be available for the boss no matter when he calls. Maybe she should send Raole out to search for Stewart. On second thought, she reasoned, it's not my problem. If Stewart is choosing to be unavailable, who am I to try to set him straight? He's surely been hired before and knows the rules. And if Stewart drops out of the picture, Jo Lee reasoned, she could be the hero with the big boss instead of remarkable Stewart. Tomorrow would be soon enough to worry about Stewart.

Now, as for the little episode tonight – was Melanie dreaming or did someone really visit her? Or maybe Melanie was just trying to be the center of attention. Jo Lee planned to watch Melanie very carefully to find out what was going on with her.

These kids might lose all privileges if they tried to outsmart old Jo Lee. She would have none of that. She wasn't particularly fond of children, and she sure wasn't going to allow one of them to even think they could outsmart her. She would be watching all of them even more carefully than before. Don't fool with Jo Lee if you know what's good for you!

CHAPTER 11

Breakfast consisted of granola bars and orange juice, but once again the children were quietly grateful. Unlike the previous evening, Jo Lee allowed the students to sit around in small groups in the dining room and large kitchen.

The dining room and kitchen both gave the impression that those who had lived in the house were just out somewhere for the day and would return. Dishes sat in cabinets and china closets. Vases and candle holders stood on sideboards and in hutches. However, the dust covering everything told a different story – one of abandonment and neglect. The students didn't seem to care or even notice the dust. They appeared to be happy to talk to each other. It was obvious that the daylight intimidated them less than the darkness of night with the light providing a means to have eye contact and get to know each other better. The sun coming through the years of dirt on the large windows still supplied a sense of grandeur as it shown into the rooms and reflected off the hanging copper pots and crystal chandeliers.

The children gathered together around the massive dining room table and at the kitchen table where many children before them had spent time eating snacks and completing homework when the mansion had once been a home full of life and love. Prior history was not on the minds of these children as they began to talk and become familiar. They were providing for Jo Lee exactly what she had planned – a means for her to stand back and observe to determine further how the children got along and what kind of personalities they had.

As she predicted, the students didn't communicate much with their assigned roommates, so she had done well in that regard, but she noticed that some of the younger boys were drawn to Melanie who continued to discuss her frightening experience last night. Jo Lee, the self-made psychologist, reasoned that this would definitely lead to conflict within the entire group, as boys would compete with each other for attention from the pretty blond and girls would become jealous. Jo Lee couldn't wait to see what would happen.

What Jo lee didn't know was that she wouldn't have to wait long. She didn't anticipate that even if students are competitive and jealous they might be able to work together toward a common goal.

For now, Jo Lee watched Darius, Max, and Benjamin listening intently as Melanie talked and giggled and flipped her long blond hair back over her shoulders with a practiced gesture. Marta began asking questions of Jo Lee about their plans for the children for the day, but Jo Lee seemed to ignore her to concentrate on the actions playing out around her.

Girls huddled in a group across the room continually stared at Melanie and then whispered behind hands to each other. What they could be saying Jo Lee only imagined, but she would bet it had everything to do with the attention Melanie seemed to be drawing with her story of the night adventure. Then, as Jo Lee leaned further around Marta to watch, the smile faded from her lips when Melanie strutted across the length of the dining room to join the very same girls who had been enjoying talking about Melanie. As Melanie approached them, the girls all smiled and began talking to her.

Now this was a novel idea for Jo Lee who stayed fairly constant in her life about whom she liked and didn't like. She didn't pretend. With Jo Lee you always knew where you stood and she didn't try to hide those feelings. Although pondering this state of the middle school interactions, Jo Lee realized that she needed to direct her attention to Marta to make plans for their first day with twenty students. They would start with a list of sizes from the children and then make a list of groceries. Having a credit card provided for them would make spending money on the children tolerable. She always enjoyed spending someone else's money.

Not being a sociable person made the entire experience of feeding more than twenty people three meals a day a challenge for Jo Lee, who was used to only taking care of herself. Marta and Raole weren't much help either, and Stewart was still not around. This job had better pay well, she thought, because playing nanny for all these kids was not her idea of fun.

Being lost in her own thoughts had blinded Jo Lee to her yet undiscovered greater challenge who was sitting quietly in a corner watching Jo Lee the entire time. Austin was pretending to be lost in his own thoughts and appeared perfectly harmless, when in reality he was plotting his next move.

CHAPTER 12

Moving the school bus to another location would have possibly drawn attention to them. Instead, it was now sitting behind the house at the edge of the woods with the license removed and the bright yellow paint now spray-painted green to blend into the bushes and trees surrounding it. Raole had risen early to begin the task of camouflaging the stolen evidence.

As Jo Lee and Marta finished their monumental lists, Raole was back in the house for the discussion about how and where to buy all these items and how to transport them back to the mansion. The reality of the situation they all faced of being in a remote location with no electricity and no transportation began to sink in. They had only obeyed orders – they hadn't questioned them. Now, how they would survive was the next great challenge the three adults recognized.

"So, have you figured it out yet?" The voice startled them all, and a few of the children visibly jumped when Stewart arrived back on the scene. Even the other adults appeared temporarily shaken before Jo Lee composed herself and then lashed out with anger toward Stewart about where he had been and why he had left without telling them. Stewart was typically a man of few words, but if pushed hard enough he had no problem expressing his feelings, just as he had on the bus when the adults were arguing. This was again one of those times. He looked Jo Lee squarely in the face and even took a step toward her, and said very loudly for all to hear, "I didn't realize that you were my boss. I suggest that if you know what's good for you, you will treat me with respect. Your survival depends on me. So, if you want to survive, you ask me nicely what I can do for you, or you can figure out on your own how to drive to pick up all the food and clothes."

There was a moment of silence in which it seemed that everyone held their breath waiting for a response from Jo Lee. This could get ugly. Jo Lee could choose to make this a battle that she might lose or a moment that would clarify in everyone's mind who was really in charge. Which would it be?

In everyone's life there will be at least one moment that will define what kind of person you are. In that moment, do you acknowledge your mistake and swallow your pride and show yourself to be a better person, or do you take a stand and argue even as you realize that you are probably wrong? This was Jo Lee's moment. Would she recognize her error or would she argue? No one could have predicted what would happen next, but all those present held their breath. Jo Lee reached out and put her hand softly on Stewart's arm, looked up into his face and smiled, "You know, Stewart, you are right. I do need to hear what you can do for us."

Stewart's surprise showed on his face, but then disappeared as Jo Lee continued to smile and waited for an answer. The children, along with Marta and Raole, almost collectively let out a sigh of relief. From where he sat, Austin thought, "That wasn't nearly as much fun as I thought it was going to be."

Still, Jo Lee waited for an answer.

"I fell asleep in the bus, but when the boss reached me on my cell phone last night he instructed me to go buy a car, which I did today with his money. I walked from here along the road, and someone stopped to ask if I wanted a ride. He took me into town where I found a car dealer and bought a fifteen-passenger van. It was much easier than I thought it would be, and we're closer to town than I thought."

Jo Lee's smile began to fade as Stewart continued, "Now, thanks to me, you'll be able to go buy food and clothes for the kids."

Jo Lee hoped that maybe the children, who now seemed busy again with their own conversations, might not have heard Stewart say that they were closer to the town than he had thought. Oh well, no reason to worry now when the children seemed to not even be paying attention. She would maybe just have to watch them more carefully. There's no way that any of them would ever think they could possibly escape, Jo Lee thought. But Jo Lee didn't really know just how much Austin was listening and thinking.

Raole and Stewart were left in charge while the two women used the van to go shopping. Marta and Jo Lee had to be very careful to not draw attention to themselves with such a large quantity of food and clothes that would be needed. They very cautiously drove further and went to two different stores to buy the clothes and only bought enough food for two days, which meant they would be returning often for more food. Buying food for twenty-five people could look suspicious if they bought too much at one time. It was probably safe to buy two bags of apples and two bags of potatoes, and three or four loaves of bread, but if they bought ten boxes of cereal and eight bags of potato chips and several cases of soda, and a dozen rolls of paper towels and toilet paper and soap at the same store, it might eventually be questioned if anyone was watching.

The kids would just have to learn to eat and live differently, Jo Lee thought, and to appreciate getting any food at all. It's not like we can order pizza and have it delivered, or take them all out for hamburgers at a fast-food restaurant. Although they had no electricity, with a gas stove she might consider making them macaroni and cheese or chili, scrambled eggs, or even hot dogs occasionally, but forget frying bacon to go with the eggs or making casseroles or oatmeal or desserts for twenty-five people. That was just out of the question. She never wanted to be a cook, and she sure wasn't going to start now. After all, peanut butter on bread was good enough for her when she was growing up.

CHAPTER 13

Raole and Stewart had explored drawers, closets, and cabinets while it was daylight to find what was there. The children were not as excited as Raole and Stewart were to find board games like Monopoly, checkers, Life, Yahtzee, Chinese checkers, and chess. There were plenty of decks of cards, jacks, and marbles. These games were not what children today in the twenty-first century found interesting. However, when children become bored, they will find delight in what is provided for them to do.

During the hours that Jo Lee and Marta shopped, the children discovered skills and the joy of teamwork that they hadn't experienced before. There were winners and losers, made-up rules, and friendly competition. Not all of the children were satisfied to not win, but none expressed anger or pouted if they lost a game. If Jo Lee had watched the interaction within the groups of children playing games, she would not have been pleased. She didn't intend for the twenty to become friends or to even get along with each other.

Therefore, Jo Lee and Marta had purchased books, cross-word puzzles, Sudoku puzzle books, and word searches with lots of pencils. Jo Lee had hoped for the children to be content to work independently and for each to spend time reading. She had not counted on the children gravitating toward each other for companionship. She was, therefore, greatly disappointed to arrive back at the mansion and see what looked like friendships developing, and she was even more frustrated as the day wore on and she witnessed the children finding ways to compete with different activities such as finding the most words in the shortest amount of time on word searches or completing a Sudoku puzzle in the shortest amount of time. If she hadn't seen it herself she would never have believed that the children even formed competitions around the card game of Solitaire to find a winner.

By mid-afternoon, Jo Lee and Marta had made over twenty peanut butter sandwiches and had given each child an apple. It was simple, but sufficiently nutritious, and thank goodness no one had a peanut allergy. Although Marta was one of those people who didn't think too deeply about whether she was happy, Jo Lee, on the other hand, did, and she was determined that she was not satisfied any longer with the current circumstance. In fact, she was becoming quite miserable about not knowing how this whole situation was going to be resolved and how much it was worth to any of them. They were getting very little communication from the person who was making decisions somewhere, and they were meantime having to do all the work taking care of these kids. And for what? What's the purpose of all this, she wondered, as she gathered trash and put food in cabinets. She became determined that if she didn't hear from him tonight, she would attempt to call him tomorrow to ask questions.

Amidst her other thoughts, Jo Lee just remembered another item that she and Marta had bought while they were out. It was a generator and gasoline that would generate electricity so that they could charge their cell phones. Where was Stewart? If he won't do anything else maybe he could at least carry in the generator before all their cell phones died. But wait, what's going on now, Jo Lee pondered as she walked through the dining room. Some of the kids are picking on Carlyle. Now this was an interesting turn of events. Never having children of her own, Jo Lee was unfamiliar with the complex nature of pre-adolescent personality traits which changed from one moment to the next. She was fascinated in this exchange of words among some of the middle-school aged students, both boys and girls.

"So Carlyle, you think you're big stuff just because you won the seventh-grade spelling bee? Anybody can spell words. I'll show you. Just give me a word," Darius said with anger in his voice.

From Sarah over in the corner, "Darius, all this because you lost at a game of checkers! Carlyle, you don't have to prove yourself. We all just need to be friends."

Not giving up on the challenge, Darius said more loudly, "Give me a word!"

From the other side of the room came a suggestion from Nadialee, "Let's have a spelling bee right now. Whoever wants to try should line up in the middle of the room."

Ever the quick-thinker, Stan posed the question, "What's the winner get?"

There was a moment before anyone said anything, and then there were more ideas than teachers at a staff meeting could have suggested.

"The winner gets to eat dinner first."

"Gets a bigger flashlight."

"Gets to take a hot shower."

"How about getting to sleep wherever you want?"

"I think the winner should get to take a walk."

"Gets to call home."

"Gets to go home!"

Now Jo Lee was paying very close attention. Was this the beginning of a mutiny? But before Jo Lee stopped their suggestions, Melanie had an idea that seemed to be accepted by everyone, possibly because it was Melanie who suggested it. "How about the winner gets to spend an afternoon alone."

Now the conversation had Austin's full attention. Darius replied for the group, "Yes. That's worth spelling for!"

CHAPTER 14

Everyone who was interested lined up in the middle of the massive living room. They found a dust-covered dictionary on a bookshelf. Jessica suggested that Jo Lee pronounce the words. For one brief moment a look of panic crossed Jo Lee's face. Someone looking on might have wondered if Jo Lee was afraid of reading words, but she quickly recovered before she thought anyone might have noticed. Austin was very perceptive, however, and he did see her reaction and interpreted it accurately.

Jo Lee said to Jessica, "You seem smart to me. You should do it."

If sarcasm was intended, Jessica ignored it and agreed to say the words that everyone else would spell. And it really did include everyone, since all of the remaining nineteen students were standing, waiting for the first word. Apparently the reward was worth the effort after being together for over twenty-four hours. An afternoon alone would seem heavenly.

The Spelling Bee began. *Curriculum. Simile. Ominous. Adjacent. Aquatic. Diary. Refugee. Canary. Jovial. Discipline.* Ten words and only two people down. This could be a long drawn-out competition, Jo Lee thought. Why couldn't they just play board games?

Soliloquy. Efficacy. Precocious. Accommodate. Belligerent. Ameliorate. Aggregate. Pernicious. Vernacular. Ubiquitous. Ten more words and five more people down. Now there were twelve still standing and the words were getting more difficult.

Another ten words – *Albatross. Fuselage. Artichoke. Rehearse. Alfalfa. Marzipan. Algorithm. Gingham. Stethoscope. Mayonnaise.* Three more competitors down. Nine to go to determine the winner. Carlyle, Austin, and Darius were among those still in the running. Not surprisingly, Jacob, Celeste, and Jessica were still standing. The three others remaining were McKenzie, Nadialee, and only one fifth-grader, Alexandria. Four boys and five girls still in it and ready to continue.

Quisling. Poinsettia. Boysenberry. Saxophone. Samaritan. Praline. Forsythia. Pasteurize. Fahrenheit. Narcissistic. After these ten words the field was narrowed to three boys: Carlyle, Austin, and

Darius. All three had a vested interest in winning –
Darius to prove a point, Carlyle to save face, and
Austin for very personal reasons. It was a part of his
plan. Austin had never really cared much about
spelling, but this spelling bee was of utmost
importance to him. His past history showed that when
he cared about something, he could put forth the effort
needed.

Carlyle got the word *sputnik*. Austin received
sauerbraten. Darius was given *edelweiss*. Each
speller was correct. Now the word was *paprika* for
Carlyle. He spelled it correctly. Austin got *wiseacre*.
He hesitated only a second about whether the e was on
wise and went on to spell it correctly. Now Darius.
He received *maelstrom*. Also correct.

Now to Carlyle. His word was *bequeath*. No
problem. Austin spelled *toboggan*. Darius was fine
with *chipotle*.

Now back to Carlyle. His word was *sayonara*. It
was fitting because he spelled it with four a's in it,
which meant he was out of the competition. He
accepted defeat with style and took a seat with the
others to watch the outcome.

Now down to two competitors and the rules
changed. If one of the remaining two students
misspelled a word and the other student spelled it
correctly, then that student would be the winner after
spelling one more word correctly. If he missed it also,

then the first speller would be given another word. The competition between the two was fierce and both looked tense.

Austin got *tsunami.* He knew that one without thinking. They had studied about it recently in science. Darius was given *thesaurus.* Again, because of English class he knew how to spell it easily.

Now *anachronism. Hippopotamus. Metamorphosis. Phenomenon.*

And then *zucchini.* Austin spelled it *zuccini*, forgetting the *h*. Everyone held their breath. Darius spelled it zuchini, getting the *h* but forgetting the second *c*. Both still remained. Now back to Austin.

Harpsichord. He got it correct. Then *archipelago* for Darius. He missed it, which meant the same word had to be spelled correctly by Austin for him to be closer to winning. Austin hesitated. In a real spelling bee he might have delayed by asking the definition and to have it used in a sentence. Both of which would have given him time to think. This wasn't a real spelling bee, but the stakes were high. An afternoon alone would give him the time he needed. He had it pronounced again and then he began letter by letter. One letter at a time to the end of the word. Darius was looking more concerned than Austin. Austin knew the word. He knew geography. He actually looked at National Geographic when he spent time in the library. And then the winner would be one word away from being determined. Austin spelled *archipelago* correctly. By the spelling bee rules, he was the winner if he correctly spelled the next word.

Austin's word was *renegade.* Again a perfect word for the speller. Austin smiled. He turned and looked at Darius as he spelled each letter to be declared the winner. Although not a friend to any of the students, there were cheers for Austin, possibly as much for him winning as having the spelling bee finally end.

Darius was not happy. Austin ignored the glares from Darius and went back to a corner of the room to sit quietly and begin his plan for an afternoon alone.

CHAPTER 15

The spelling bee had taken up all that remained of the afternoon, and now it was time to prepare dinner. Jo Lee felt like all she was doing was going from one meal to the next preparing food for too many people. As she found pots and pans in the large kitchen, she said to Marta, "These kids need to start doing chores! I had to when I was young and it didn't hurt me!"

Despite her earlier run-in with Stewart, she wondered where he and Raole were. They seemed to never be around for the cooking and cleaning. And now that she was feeling negative about the situation, she expressed her thoughts to Marta as they boiled water for macaroni and opened huge cans of green beans.

"You know, I've been thinking about what we're involved in here and I wonder why these kids have been kidnapped. We've been given no explanation about when whoever's in charge of this will get these kids and when they will pay us. Next time he calls I want answers."

Marta said very little because she didn't really have an opinion. She was one of those people who was blessed with a cooperative spirit. All her life Marta had just done what she was told without questioning why or how it would benefit her. She was obedient and grateful to know that she would be well-paid for her efforts.

As Jo Lee continued to complain and question who might be responsible for their circumstances and what would he do if she went to the police now, and what she would do with the money promised to them, she was unaware of Austin standing at the doorway. Jo Lee's mind began to race – how long had he been standing there? How much had he heard? Austin, a master of deception, put a look on his face of complete innocence and said, "Oh wow, I love macaroni and cheese! I was just wondering when I might get my afternoon alone for winning the spelling bee."

Was Jo Lee fooled into believing that Austin hadn't heard her discussion? Not for a minute, but she was as good at hiding her true thoughts as Austin was. They were truly a match for each other. Turning on what charm she could fake, as she had when backed into a corner by Stewart, Jo Lee said, "Well, Austin, we'll have to see about that."

Not to be out-done, Austin smiled sweetly while saying as he walked away, "Okay. Thanks for talking to me. Dinner smells good."

Jo Lee watched as Austin walked through the dining room and back into the living room where the children were in groups still talking and laughing. She stood where she was by the stove, not moving and not making eye contact with Marta. Jo Lee recognized her mistake, but wondered if Austin had heard any useable information. He had acted completely unaware of over-hearing any conversation. After all, he was a 7th-grade boy. How much of what he had heard could make sense to him or mean anything to him? What had she been saying or had already said that he could have heard from the dining room if he had been standing there listening for a while?

She couldn't have said names. She didn't know any names to tell. When she received phone calls from the person running the show her phone said "unknown caller," so there was no name. But, Austin might have heard her complaining about not knowing details like who was controlling them and why were the children involved, and how long would this go on. If he had heard her questions, would it matter? So what if Austin knew she was frustrated about the situation.

Did that make a difference? In typical Jo Lee style when she knew she was wrong, she decided that none of this was relevant because Austin was wrong for walking in on them while they were cooking and talking. He should have stayed with the other children, but instead he got nosey and now he would have to be punished. She was good at punishments. He would be sorry that he had intruded on her private conversation.

Austin, on the other hand, was sitting in the midst of the other nineteen with thoughts of his own. Jo Lee might think she could control him, but he now knew that there was someone else really in charge, and he knew that person would be quite interested to know that Jo Lee was playing both sides to make the most money and turn the person in charge into the police to save herself if that was necessary. Now that was valuable information worth having.

CHAPTER 16

Liz Rollins took care of things in their home and in their marriage. Her husband, Mark Rollins, was so busy with work as a middle-school principal that she was forced to make decisions for both of them regarding their three children and running the house, including the finances. She wanted the best for her family and for herself – the best house on the block, expensive cars, stylish clothes, membership in the best club and gym, the right group of friends for her children, and people with connections and money to be with for social events. All this cost money, and a school principal didn't make enough for it all. She was far too busy to bother getting a job herself, so credit cards became the solution. The more credit card purchases she made, the more offers that came in the mail to get more credit cards. It didn't take long before her expensive habits caught up with her. She had always been able to juggle paying on one by taking out cash on another and borrowing money from the savings account and the children's college funds – until now. It was now a serious problem with too many credit cards that were at their limit and with no money to pay on them with the savings gone and the college funds empty. Mark was unaware of any of this, because on payday he got enough cash to buy gasoline and occasionally a cup of coffee, and deposited the majority of his check into the checking account, not realizing how quickly it was gone again.

Then one day while surfing the Internet, Liz discovered on-line gambling. She started small and then risked more and more. Every time she played she felt lucky. She would think constantly that the next hand would be the one that would win it all back for her. Okay, well maybe the next one. She couldn't quit now because what if the next hand would be the one that would pay off all her debt before her husband knew they were about to lose their house, cars, club memberships, and their friends. She thought that no one would want to spend time with them when they had lost everything. She couldn't imagine a life without everything she had now. So now she was obsessed with getting that next big hand. She didn't have time to prepare dinner or pick up the children from school. They could ride the bus home like other kids. It wouldn't hurt them. The house could wait to be cleaned. The dust would still be there tomorrow after she made her money back and had enough to pay off all the bills and put back the money into savings and the college funds and pay the membership fees and the car and house payments. It would all be okay.

So when Mark came home late last night after the worst day of his career, Liz was too busy on the computer to talk with him. There would be time for talking, she reasoned, after everything was put back and paid back and her life was perfect again.

Maybe then she would tell him about the phone calls she had started getting. When this was all settled and they were sitting on the beach on vacation watching the children occupying themselves in the ocean, they would share a good laugh together about how close they had come to losing everything, including their integrity. But for right now there was nothing to laugh about when Mark came home late and stressed, and his wife was too busy to talk with him about phone calls or finances.

The first phone call to Liz had come about a week ago. Apparently there are people out there watching for desperate victims like Liz who have fallen into serious debt and need a way out. A week ago it had seemed easy to agree to go along with their plan while she was still trying to make back all her lost money. Then the next phone call gave more details that began to make it all seem possible. All she had to do was provide details about her husband and the middle school and the school board. The deal was that these callers would end up with four million dollars and she would get a million to pay everything back and even have some extra money. She could actually make money with this plan. It sounded too good to be true, but they said they would take care of everything now that she had given them all the information they needed. What harm was there in telling them about the school? After all, they said that if the school board cooperated no one would be hurt. Surely the board could easily spare five million dollars from a big school system like this one. They wouldn't even feel the loss of the money the way she was feeling it in her life.

Mark seemed so busy with work that she hadn't even talked to him last night when he came home and now he was back at work today. They hadn't talked this morning because she was busy getting their children ready for school when he had left. So, maybe everything is okay and it was all being taken care and she would just end up with her money and no one would even know what was going on. She realized that she had been so worried about their finances lately that she hadn't even taken time to watch television. Now with her cup of coffee in her hand she turned on the news to catch up with the world since she believed that everything in her life was going to be okay. But when the news came on, it was as though her world stopped and she knew she was involved in something much bigger than she had ever imagined.

CHAPTER 17

After dinner the twenty children seemed restless in the mansion. Jo Lee suggested that about half of them take baths tonight and the other half could have baths in the morning. Not many of the children seemed anxious to cooperate with this idea, but when Jo Lee explained that there were two choices – either take a bath tonight or help with laundry and dishes – it seemed that all the children wanted to take baths all of a sudden. To determine who would help Jo Lee and who would take baths, they each pulled out a slip of paper from a bowl that had either *bath* or *laundry* written on it.

It wouldn't be dark until around eight o'clock, so the ten boys and girls who were to take baths went upstairs to gather what they needed from the piles of toiletries that Jo Lee and Marta had bought. They picked out new clothes to put on while their clothes were being washed. The ten children helping Jo Lee and Marta were getting the dirty clothes together to begin washing them.

Stewart and Raole had been installing the generator at the same time that Jo Lee had been complaining about them. The generator efficiently ran on natural gas on the property and then supplied the electricity that they needed. There were still very few lights that worked, but having hot water for bathing, cooking, and laundry would provide them comfort. Although the evenings were cool in the fall, they should be able to get by for now without having heat in the old mansion.

Austin was one of the children helping with the laundry and dishes. He offered to gather dirty clothes because that would give him a chance to explore. Jo Lee handed him a large basket, which he took and started to walk through the dining room. It was then that he glanced over and saw a phone plugged into a charger lying on a table in the corner. He guessed that it belonged to Jo Lee. Would she miss it if he slipped it into his pocket as he looked like he was just gathering dirty clothes? He decided it was worth it to see who might answer on the other end.

All he would have to do is go to the log and call back who might have called Jo Lee last night. Plus, that would show him a phone number where that person could be reached. Austin thought whoever it is must have something to do with the children being kidnapped from school since Austin had overheard Jo Lee say to Marta that the next time the person called she would ask questions.

So, all he had to do now was disappear with the phone for just a few minutes. Jo Lee would never even notice. He walked on through the dining room and looked around as if searching for dirty clothes. Then Austin continued to stay aware that Jo Lee was not following him while walking through the living room and up the stairs as he was whistling and glancing around.

At the top of the steps he started down the hall and yelled out to the girls, "Anyone with dirty clothes throw them out into the hall!" Then he went further down the hall and yelled, "Hey, guys! Throw your dirty clothes into the hall!" A few did and some yelled out, "Just a minute!"

Austin looked toward both ends of the hall and seeing no one, he set down the basket in the middle and ran toward the boys' end of the hallway and slipped down a set of steps that he suspected would lead him down into the dining room. He had guessed right, which he discovered as he quickly maneuvered the steps while watching the doorway to the kitchen for Jo Lee to appear. At the bottom of the steps he could hear her voice in the living room instructing one of the children about how to sort the books. That would give him just a few seconds to make it from the bottom of these steps over to the corner and unplug the phone and slip it into his pocket.

Staying aware of the direction of Jo Lee's voice, he made it to the table when he heard someone coming from the kitchen. Although it wasn't Jo Lee, anyone might wonder why he was picking a cell phone up off the table. It was Stan and Jessica. They were obviously so taken with each other that they didn't even look in Austin's direction. He was not of any significance to them compared to their feelings for each other, so he just blended into the surroundings.

As soon as they left the dining room, his hand reached out to grab the cell phone while his other hand pulled on the cord to unplug it. He was so close. His hand closed around the phone and tugged on the cord to unplug it.

He could hear Jo Lee's voice. Where was she? He had been so focused on getting the phone that he had lost track of where she was. He couldn't afford that kind of mistake. It would only take one time catching him doing something for her not to trust him. Then she would never let him out of her sight.

He held his breath, but then heard one of the girls in the living room ask Jo Lee where to put the games. Bless her.

He grabbed the phone and heard the cord hit the floor under the tables as he took two steps at a time to the second floor, scooping up dirty clothes from the floor outside a few doors, while running toward the basket and slipping the phone into his pocket. In one fluid movement he picked up the basket and ran into his room and closed the door.

Fortunately he found his room to be empty. Apparently Zackary and Cameron weren't chosen to bathe or they were in the hall or bathroom. He locked the bedroom door so he wouldn't be interrupted and then moved across the bedroom near the window for better reception. He couldn't waste time. As planned, he went to the phone log and saw the last number that had called Jo Lee. He touched the number and Call Mobile and heard the phone ringing. He waited, almost anticipating that no one would answer and not knowing what he would say if he left a message.

So, he was surprised to hear a male voice answer and say, "Why are you calling me? I thought I had made it clear that you were not to call me. Hello? Jo Lee, what's going on?"

Austin sat quietly, listening and daring not to even breathe. The person at the other end was obviously surprised and angry about getting the call. Austin hesitated, but his whispered message to the man on the other end of the phone was simple, "Don't trust Jo Lee."

"What? Why not?" The voice was now loud and impatient as he continued, "Who is this? Believe me, we'll figure out who you are and then there will be no mercy shown for you. Sorry about your luck!"

Then Austin heard a click. He needed one more minute, but as he was getting ready to dial 9-1-1, he heard Jo Lee calling his name, and she sounded close. He wouldn't know what to tell anyone who answered at 9-1-1 about how to get to where he was anyway.

CHAPTER 18

He didn't have time. Now he had to get the phone back without Jo Lee seeing him. He at least knew a number now where the person could be reached and he would not forget it.

He slid the phone back into his pocket and unlocked the door with the basket under one arm. Again watching for Jo Lee, he went down the back stairway. Too late. He could hear her yelling in the kitchen, "Where's my phone? Who has my phone?"

With Jo Lee's voice coming closer, Austin quickly moved across the room to the table and pulled the phone from his pocket, plugged it into the cord, and left it lying under the table. Then he slipped out of the dining room into the living room and stood at the bottom of the living room steps waiting to hear what would happen next.

He didn't have long to wait. Jo Lee and Marta both went from the kitchen into the dining room with Marta talking, "Are you sure it didn't just fall on the floor? Maybe it was on the edge of the table and it just fell off."

Jo Lee and Marta leaned down at the same time and saw the phone under the table. Marta said, "See? It was there all along."

The scowl on Jo Lee's face showed that she didn't believe it, while she explained, "I'm sure I looked all around this table and only saw the cord under it. It may be getting dark in here, but I know what I saw!"

Marta's response, "Well you have it now," did not reassure Jo Lee that there wasn't something suspicious going on. Jo Lee walked across the floor and into the living room and saw Austin at the bottom of the living room steps looking as if he had just been coming down from upstairs carrying the basket of dirty clothes.

He couldn't help himself from asking, "Everything okay? You look upset. What should I do with these dirty clothes?"

He was too cool, Jo Lee decided. He always had a look on his face that attempted to be innocent but made him look even more suspicious. He wasn't fooling her with that Mr. Innocent look. What had he been up to? When she found out, he would be extremely sorry, and it was only a matter of time before she would be finding out.

Kuhns

CHAPTER 19

Starting the laundry and getting half of the children to take baths felt like a major accomplishment to Jo Lee. She was tired. She yelled for Raole and Stewart and told them that it was time to get the kids in their bedrooms and this time, she informed them, they would all be put in their rooms with no flashlights. She didn't want any more "Shenanigans like last night!" They had better all stay in their rooms tonight and sleep quietly because, "I don't want to hear you!"

So, the men walked the boys up to their rooms and made sure they had gathered all of their flashlights because they didn't want to make Jo Lee any angrier than she already was. Jo Lee and Marta gathered the girls' flashlights. No one argued. They could all see that Jo Lee was not happy, so the quicker they were in their rooms, the faster they could be away from her.

Now in their bedroom was Austin's opportunity to talk to Cameron. In the growing darkness, he watched until Zackary had been quiet long enough that he might be asleep. Austin whispered out into the room, "Cameron, are you awake?"

Cameron nodded, but then realized that Austin couldn't see him, and said, "Yea, I'm awake."

Austin seized the chance and said, "Cameron, I want to talk to you about something. Can I come over there closer to you so I don't have to talk so loud?"

Cameron said, "Okay."

Showing unusual concern, Austin said, "Are you sure you can stay awake?"

Cameron replied that he could, so Austin got out of his own bed and moved slowly across the room in the dark and sat on the floor beside Cameron's bed. Just as Austin opened his mouth to talk, they heard Jo Lee screaming, "Whoever had my phone is going to suffer! You think you got away with it, but don't think for a minute that you did. And until I figure out which one of you used the phone, you're all going to be locked in your rooms. And if one of you doesn't confess, you're all going to be sorry!"

They could hear Jo Lee coming closer as she stomped through the hallway yelling. Cameron began to whimper. Austin whispered, "It's going to be okay. Don't cry. She won't hurt you."

But Cameron had been close to tears since getting on the bus in front of the school. Now sobs escaped through his mouth.

Jo Lee, now even angrier because she could hear Cameron sobbing, swung open their door and screamed, "Quit crying! You're not a baby!"

With the light from the flashlight she saw Austin sitting on the floor beside Cameron's bed. She came closer.

"What do you think you're doing? I can see through your innocence. You're not fooling me. Get in your bed and stay there. Tomorrow I will deal with you!"

With that she slammed the door closed and locked it with a key from the outside, which caused Cameron to cry harder. Again Jo Lee yelled, "I told you to quit crying!"

Cameron covered his head with his pillow. Zackary must have been really tired, because even with Jo Lee's yelling and slamming the door and Cameron crying, no sound came from him.

Although Austin had moved back to his bed when he was told to by Jo Lee, he now quietly crept back to the side of Cameron's bed and whispered, "Cameron, it will be okay."

Cameron was now even more afraid than he had been when Jo Lee was screaming at him. He was afraid that Jo Lee would come back in at any moment and find Austin beside him and blame him for it.

He begged Austin between sobs, "Please leave me alone. I don't want to get into trouble. Please don't hurt me."

Caught by surprise at Cameron's words, Austin whispered, "Cameron, I'm not going to hurt you. I want you to help us get away from here."

Cameron paused between sobs, "What?"

Austin said, "I need your help to get us out of here."

Cameron now felt confused as well as scared, but could hear in Austin's voice something that made him begin to calm down and listen. "You can help us get out of here. You'll be a hero and your mother will be so proud of you. Here's what you need to do."

CHAPTER 20

"Hey! We need out of here to go to the bathroom!" Zackary had tried to go out the door and found that they were locked in. Cameron was awake, but stayed very quiet on his bed. Austin joined Zackary in yelling to try to summon Jo Lee.

Instead it was Raole who showed up. "What's all the noise about?"

Zackary replied, "Jo Lee locked us all in our rooms last night. When we get out of here we're going to complain to human services!"

Austin wondered if Zackary was trying to be humorous or was being serious about calling human services after this was over because of being locked in their rooms. If they ever did get away from there they would all just be so grateful to be back home and away from crazy Jo Lee that being locked in would be just one of the many complaints they would have for anyone who would listen.

Raole commented, "Why would she lock you in? I'm afraid she's losing her grip on reality. If I were you boys I would just stay out of her way because she's already on the warpath this morning and, believe me, someone's going to pay the price for making her mad. My advice is to do what she says and stay away from her."

Not to be intimidated by Raole and his advice, Austin said, "She owes half of us a bath today. It's only fair that we get it because we're the ones who did all the work last night."

Raole's response was not promising, "I'll mention it to her, but I'm telling you, stay out of her way if you know what's good for you. Before this day is over someone is going to be plenty miserable if Jo Lee has anything to do with it." With that being said, Raole went on down the hall to finish unlocking bedroom doors.

Raole's statements did nothing to reassure Cameron, who was still lying on his bed listening to the discussion. He just wanted to go home. He wanted away from this place and back to the safety of his life with his parents. When he left for school two days ago he never imagined that he might not ever be home again. The longer he laid there and thought about it, the sadder he became. And with these thoughts, Cameron's tears started. At first there were slow, quiet tears drizzling their way down his cheeks. Then hiccups started from trying to hold in the sobs that were now filling the room.

Austin thought, wow, this kid is good. I would even believe his tears are real. It occurred to Austin for only a brief second that maybe Cameron really was upset and wasn't pretending, but that didn't stop Austin from yelling down the hall, "Hey! Someone needs to come in here to help Cameron. He's in a lot of pain!"

Within seconds children came to their door. Jessica and Celeste were the first to be by Cameron's side.

"Cameron, what's wrong?"

Now Cameron's sobs could be heard out in the hallway where more children were gathering, all stretching their necks and standing on their toes to see in the room and find out what was happening.

More voices joined Austin's in yelling for the adults. Finally, Jo Lee's voice could be heard above the rest, "Get away from that door and get downstairs for breakfast or you won't get any!"

All but Austin and Cameron cleared the hall fast and made their way to the steps and down to breakfast below. Since eating seemed to be their only chance at survival, they couldn't pass it up. They knew without a doubt that if they missed a meal they would have to wait until the next one was provided because Jo Lee allowed no snacking between meals. And no one – except Austin – was brave enough to disobey Jo Lee, as he was doing now by remaining with Cameron.

"He's in pain and he can't tell me where it hurts. Maybe since you're a woman like his mom he'll be able to tell you. He seemed to have woken up in pain this morning."

Jo Lee, not falling for Austin's attempt to make her feel motherly, growled, "Well, there's nothing I can do about it. He needs to go eat breakfast now or he won't get any."

Austin, staying calm and sounding sweet, looked at Cameron and then at Jo Lee with a completely baffled expression before saying, "Cameron can hardly breathe. How's he going to eat? He's in too much pain to even talk."

"I said he needs to go eat. Now get up out of bed and go downstairs to eat."

Cameron, possibly out of real fear now, tried to stand up but grabbed his stomach and fell back onto the bed, sobbing and hyperventilating while trying to catch his breath.

Austin was now showing some frustration. "How can you yell at him when he's obviously in pain? You've got to do something!"

Jo Lee was now equally becoming agitated. Having sympathy for anyone went way beyond any human characteristics she might have, and she certainly didn't feel sorry for this little boy who was crying instead of telling her where it hurt.

"Cameron. Tell me what hurts or I'm going to physically carry you down those steps and make you eat."

Now even Austin wondered how far Jo Lee would go to win a battle. She probably could carry poor Cameron down the steps the way he was now, weak and fearful.

Much to Austin's surprise and disappointment, Cameron stood up and took a few steps, at first slowly and then more quickly, as Jo Lee stood over him with a scowl on her face, glaring at him as he moved his way toward the door. Turning to Austin, Jo Lee said, "See. I knew there was nothing wrong with him. I ought to just lock you in this room for always being involved in something. You're up to no good and I know it."

As Cameron neared the doorway, he slowed again to reach out to steady himself, but with one movement Austin was by his side with his arm around Cameron's shoulders to help him down the hall, both of them ignoring Jo Lee, who again showed no sympathy with her words, "He can walk by himself. Don't baby him."

Although close behind the two boys, Jo Lee was unable to hear Austin's whispered message to

Cameron over the voices of the other children in the dining room, as they walked slowly down the steps side by side, "You can do this. Don't give up. Just keep thinking of seeing your mom and dad."

CHAPTER 21

When they were finishing eating breakfast Jo Lee began dictating orders about what everyone would be doing before lunch. Those who had not taken a bath the night before would be taking one this morning. The rest of the children would be gathering dirty clothes and washing dishes under the supervision of Marta. Jo Lee wouldn't be taking any chances – she would be watching upstairs to be sure everyone was doing what they were supposed to be doing. There would be no further drama.

Before they got away from the table, Celeste started a discussion that Jo Lee had hoped would not come up. "Hey you guys, have you all wondered if there are ghosts here?"

All of a sudden children immediately paid attention. Alexandria's eyes grew larger as Julianna explained what she had read in a journal she had found on a shelf in the living room. "Now I know they meant this house! There's stories about this house in a journal in the living room that tells about seeing ghosts here and all the things that have happened here through the years. This house has been here over a hundred and fifty years. In fact, it was here during the Civil War and when West Virginia became a state in 1863. The first story is about a woman named Emmeline, who lived in this house with her husband and four children. One night when it was dark she heard her husband calling her name outside in the back yard. But he was away in the Civil War, so he couldn't really have been out there. She left the children in the house and told them she was going outside to see their father. Emmeline went into the backyard, following her husband's voice as he called to her, and she tripped over a root in the dark. She fell down the hill and hit her head on a rock and died. Now people have said that sometimes in the dark in the backyard you can hear her husband calling her name - Emmeline."

Not to be outdone, Jacob contributed to the story-telling, "I read the journal too and found a story about a man named Hiram from back in the 1890's who lived here with a house full of kids and relatives. One night he was upstairs and went into the attic on some steps that pull down. They said he was getting an old dollhouse to bring down for the girls to play with. So he carried it down the steps and put it in one of the bedrooms. Then he went back up for the dollhouse furniture and brought it all down in a box. And then he made one more trip up the steps to find a box with dollhouse people, but he never came back down. He just disappeared somewhere up there in the attic. They say on some nights you can hear him walking around up there and up and down the steps and you can see that the dollhouse furniture has been moved around in the dollhouse."

By this time not just Alexandria looked a little frightened. Caitlin and Max were looking around to see reactions from the older children, who obviously were not sure how much truth there was in these ghost tales. Stan was the first to react. "Let's think about it. Has anybody heard anything suspicious?"

Lauren, who rarely spoke up, said, "I heard it. Last night I heard it. Caitlin, you heard it too. I asked you last night if you were over by the dollhouse when we were in bed, and you said that you were in bed. Julianna and Jessica, did you get out of bed last night?"

Julianna and Jessica both shook their heads and Jessica said, "I heard someone walking around in the room and I figured it was one of you."

Now Carlyle got involved. "I heard someone walking in the hall last night."

Zackary added quickly, "That was Jo Lee."

No one was sure whether to laugh or not. Zackary said, "No, really. Jo Lee locked us in our rooms last night."

No one said anything. Discussions about Jo Lee were scary enough without thinking about ghosts and being locked in rooms. Alexandria started to physically tremble. Melanie went to her and put her arm around her shoulder. "Don't worry. Zachary's just kidding."

"No, I'm not," Zackary said. "We were locked in and I had to yell for Jo Lee to let me out to go to the bathroom."

Melanie shot Zackary a look that said to be quiet and even it's true to stop saying it. Zackary took the hint, but Austin seized the chance to ask Jo Lee, who had heard enough while she was in the kitchen to come back in the dining room ready to stop the children from any further discussion of ghosts and locked doors.

"Hey, Jo Lee, can I have my afternoon alone this afternoon for winning the spelling bee?"

Jo Lee responded, "No, I don't know about that."

Not to be put off, Austin persisted, "I won fair and square. When do I get my free afternoon?"

Jo Lee ignored him and told the children it was time to take baths and do chores.

Austin did not like to be ignored.

CHAPTER 22

North Middle School had been in session yesterday as it was again today. It was important to attempt to maintain a feeling of normalcy so that the students would continue to learn and not be afraid.

Attending classes was anything but normal, however. When the buses unloaded in the front of the building the students were escorted across the concrete courtyard into the school by teachers and policemen and board office staff to assure the safety of each student. Although the media was kept at a safe distance from the front door, they were all there with their cameras and microphones, hoping to catch a glimpse or a few words that indicated that the students were nervous.

There wasn't much of an opportunity for exaggerating news from the school with the escorts and limited access to administrators. No one was permitted to talk to the news media except Superintendent Bernard, and he wasn't talking much. He kept his conversations brief even with School Board members and the principal, Mr. Mark Rollins. The superintendent had come to North Middle yesterday, the first full day without twenty students, and met with the staff before the students arrived. Then an assembly was held in which he reassured the students that they were safe at the school and that it was important for them to continue to study and leave the concerns to the adults to take care of.

This reassurance obviously did not get heard by the students who were not there. Attendance was down. Parents didn't necessarily buy into the idea that their children would be safe at school. After all, twenty students had just been driven away on a bus from North Middle School and never returned. Their children were gone. It was unheard of and something like they had never experienced before. Students don't get kidnapped from schools. Security cameras and locked doors are supposed to prevent that.

The parents didn't mind talking to the media, but they had little information to offer. However, that didn't stop reporters from interviewing parents who vented their frustration at the school system and the principal and the kidnappers. Some parents were in tears when describing saying good-bye to their children two days ago with the expectation that they would return home from school as they always did. But not this time. This time their children were just gone and in the hands of some scary people. They didn't know if they would get to celebrate their children's next birthdays or see them graduate some day from high school. Those dreams might be gone for those twenty parents.

Then there were those parents and members of the community who were very angry that something like this could ever happen. They paid their tax dollars and expected their children to be protected. They were in PTO and athletic boosters and came to parent conferences. How could something like this happen? And always the question that remained unanswered: How could the principal allow something like this to happen? Wasn't he taught how to handle these types of situations? How could he have just gathered twenty students and handed them over to possible terrorists?

Mr. Rollins was still himself unaware how this could have happened. But Liz Rollins knew, or at least she was beginning to figure it out.

After beginning to see the news coverage, it occurred to Liz how she was involved. Her dilemma now was whether to tell Mark now or ever. Would it help him to know? Would it help the police or FBI find the children? Probably not with these hoodlums that she was dealing with. They had no scruples, no morals, and no heart. They were all about money and getting it any way possible, including kidnapping children.

She convinced herself that she wasn't a bad person. She had only gotten caught up with people who were bad. She believed that she was just a victim. The bad people were taking advantage of her unfortunate circumstances. But no matter how much she tried to believe that she wasn't guilty of any wrongdoing, the more she worried that something might actually happen to those twenty kids and she would be responsible. Again the thought, should she tell Mark?

Mark Rollins was having a hard time being a principal and maintaining his calm demeanor. Everywhere he turned he felt more stress. The phone at the school rang continually with openly hostile callers that Miss Johnson tried to subdue or refer to Mr. Rollins and the Board of Education. There was no good answer to tell anyone. No, they didn't know anything more than they knew from the first day. No, they had not been contacted by kidnappers. No, they had no signs of terrorism at the school. No, the principal hadn't been fired.

CHAPTER 23

It was Austin's turn to take a bath. He couldn't pass it up because he didn't know when the opportunity would come again. Bathing and putting on clean clothes occupied him for a little while, but his mind kept active about where the pull-down steps were and how he could get to the attic without being seen.

CHAPTER 24

It wasn't supposed to happen like this. The phone call from the kid on Jo Lee's phone proved to him that these kids were too smart for their own good. Now he couldn't wait, as he had planned, for the school superintendent to be so desperate that the school system would do anything to get these kids back. He would just have to count on the school board seeing the wisdom of doing the right thing to get these kids back safely and in one piece. So now it was time to make the phone call.

He called the cell phone of Superintendent Bernard and said what he wanted to say in only a few seconds – just long enough to make his demands known. "Listen carefully. Five million dollars needs to be deposited into a bank account within two days.

For each day there is a delay one child will not be returned. I'll call later with the account number."

His communication with Jo Lee last night showed him her frustration with the children and with the situation. He had thought she was the perfect person to handle this job, but her emotional state seemed to deteriorate quickly. After only two days she was falling apart. And Marta, Stewart, and Raole didn't seem capable of taking over. They were obviously just along for the ride and to get a big paycheck at the end. It was time for this to be over. It was just that simple. Give him the money he needed to pay off Mrs. Rollins and then he was finished with this job.

He didn't value human life. He had no family and was raised in an orphanage. He didn't really care one way or the other what happened to these twenty children. He didn't understand the love families had for each other. He didn't need that. He was tough and alone, and that's the way he needed to be. No emotional ties. No time spent on things like birthdays and holidays and family time. He hadn't had those experiences all his life and he certainly didn't need to waste time now feeling sorry for other people who might lose those they love.

Those kids were victims of circumstances. They were in the wrong place at the wrong time. Who knew why the principal picked the kids that he chose. It was just their misfortune to have been selected. Now they would suffer the consequences if Superintendent Bernard didn't take his demands seriously.

As for Jo Lee, Marta, Stewart, and Raole, they needed to just follow orders or they could be eliminated, too. It would be easier to get rid of them than to have to listen to Jo Lee whine or to have to pay them big for this job. He had no loyalties to anyone. They could all be replaced.

CHAPTER 25

"Five million dollars! They want five million dollars! Where do we get five million dollars?" Superintendent Bernard was now relaying the information to the Board President from the phone call he had received.

Mr. Bernard continued to vent his frustration. "They could just as well demand ten thousand or twenty million. It wouldn't be any more difficult or easier than asking for five million dollars. We don't have it. And even if we did, we couldn't just hand it over to someone, even to someone who had our students. It's completely unreasonable. Who do they think they are making that kind of demand? Well, too bad. They're not getting it."

On the other hand the Board President felt like Superintendent Bernard was being unreasonable.

"Look, Mr. Bernard, we really don't have a choice. Max Sterling is one of those children and we owe it to him and to all those other students and parents to do whatever we can to get them safely home, even if it means borrowing the money to make it happen."

Mr. Bernard started to object again, but the Board President raised his hand as if to stop whatever the superintendent's argument was going to be.

The Board President continued, "Now, I say we start making phone calls to come up with money before we have to find out if they're serious or not about not returning our children. I suggest we start with John Sterling to tell him about how we can get his son Max back and then we'll call the other board members. We'll need to call Mark Rollins because he should hear the demands from us and not from some reporter. And then you need to call someone form the media – whoever you think – to give them the right story so they don't blow it out of proportion. You know how easily they can do that. Also, you need to call the police in case they don't already know what the demands are."

"Well, most importantly," Mr. Bernard added to the discussion, "I need to start talking to our finance director to see how we can give away five million dollars."

The Board President replied, "No, Mr. Bernard, the most important thing is getting all of those twenty children back here safe and sound."

CHAPTER 26

Austin didn't know how much time he had to investigate. At any moment Jo Lee might notice his absence. She seemed to stay aware of where Austin was more than the other students. He could hear voices at a distance, but they mingled with the sounds of water running for bathing and of children talking behind closed doors in the bedrooms. Half of the children were again helping Jo Lee and Marta with chores. It should be safe to look around.

He started in the hallway looking up at the ceiling for the pull-down steps. It was a long hallway. Could they be in one of the bedrooms instead of the hallway? Anything was possible in this old house. There could even be walls in different places since the time the ghost story was written. Maybe in a closet. Maybe instead of real steps it might be a ladder that wouldn't take a lot of space. So, he wondered, does that mean I have to look in every closet? He started to look in a few of the rooms not being used. No luck. Could the steps have been taken away altogether? Maybe there was no way into the attic anymore. He couldn't rule out the possibility that the steps might be in one of the bedrooms that was being used.

Then, just as he heard voices coming up the stairway from the living room he spotted a cut-out square with a rope hanging from it in a corner of the last bedroom closest to the boys' bathroom. Now he quickly closed that door and walked toward the voices at the opposite end of the hall. He had found what he wanted.

One of the children was Ryan, who was friendly toward everyone. "Hey, Austin, how ya' doing?"

Austin acknowledged the greeting with a thumbs-up.

Nadialee said, "Austin, congrats on the spelling bee. You're good."

Austin mumbled, "Thanks," but kept walking toward the steps. Now to make his presence known so that Jo Lee wouldn't come searching for him.

He found her showing some of the children how to hand-wash clothes and run the gas dryer. Marta was washing dishes while some of the children were drying.

Raole was making adjustments to the ancient hot water tank commenting that they would be lucky if it lasted. Stewart was not in sight. That seemed pretty typical

Just so Jo Lee would know he was around, he walked into the laundry area and asked Jo Lee what was for lunch. Her glare preceded her response, "Maybe you should help fix it, Austin, and then you'd know what we're having."

Not to be shown up, Austin smiled and said, "I'd love to help. Can I go see what we have so I'll know what to cook?"

Jo Lee gave him one of her looks in which she squeezed her eyes almost closed and pursed her lips. He wondered what was coming next.

Jo Lee took a deep breath, as if it pained her to refrain from speaking her real thoughts, and said, "Sure, Austin. Go see what you can cook."

CHAPTER 27

Helping to prepare a salad and cheese sandwiches had kept Austin busy for the rest of the morning. Lunch had gone smoothly with the children discussing the possibility of real ghosts and how terrified they would be after dark if they heard a voice calling "Emmeline," or if they heard someone walking up and down pull-down steps somewhere in the house.

Just as lunch was winding down, Cameron started moaning and grabbing his stomach.

Jo Lee, typically unsympathetic toward anyone's needs, just looked at Cameron as he continued to clutch his stomach and groan.

Cameron put his hands on either side of his head and groaned again, which caused Jo Lee to become even less sympathetic. "So, which is it, Cameron, your stomach or your head?"

"It's both. I feel like I'm going to throw up and pass out."

"Well, let's get you to your bedroom so you can sleep."

"No!" Cameron quickly answered. "I can't walk up the steps. I hurt all over. Can I just lie on the couch?"

Jo Lee looked skeptical, but his tears started, and Cameron looked and sounded pathetic. Surely even Jo Lee would want to help Cameron in any way possible.

And it worked. Stan and Jessica jumped up to help him to the couch with Cameron starting to sob. Jo Lee actually began to look a little distraught. She'd never taken care of anybody sick before and didn't think she wanted to start now.

But Austin saw that between cleaning up after lunch and being uncertain about what to do for Cameron, Jo Lee would be occupied, which would give him time that he needed to take care of something.

With everyone busy either cleaning up lunch or doing laundry, or sitting with Cameron, Austin took advantage of being alone and slipped up the back steps of the dining room to the second floor. He quickly found the room with the pull-down steps and went in and closed the door. Although this wasn't his original plan, it would have to do. He had wanted his alone-time for winning the spelling bee to have time to just slip away to go find help, but there was not enough time for that now since Jo Lee wasn't giving him his afternoon alone. She could come looking for him at any moment. He had to develop an alternative plan.

It had been great timing to hear that the house had an attic while they were telling ghost stories this morning. He would explore the attic and see what it had to offer for him to be able to get out of the house undetected. He knew he couldn't just walk out a door because Jo Lee would know immediately since the doors were constantly being watched on the outside by Raole and Stewart.

He just hoped that Cameron could keep up the sick act. Austin also hoped that once he had this figured out, he wouldn't be locked in his room tonight or he wouldn't be able to carry out his plan.

Now he needed to pull down the steps. The rope was long enough, but it took a lot of strength to pull down on it. He had not expected the thud that happened when the bottom step hit the floor. Now he paused to be sure that no one came to check out the noise. He waited, listening closely for approaching steps or voices, but no one came.

Now to get up the stairs and see if the steps could close from above. It was difficult to quietly ascend the steps because they creaked and bumped the floor with each step he took. But, he reached the top and then looked around for a magic way to close the steps from above. Even with the light from the windows in the room below, he couldn't see how it would be possible, and had decided that he would just have to take a chance and hope to not be discovered, when he finally saw it. It was a pulley system that again took strength but worked to pull the steps up from below and close them so that no one below would ever detect that someone had gone into the attic.

He was now in almost complete darkness, and would have to remember tonight to bring a flashlight. For now there was an attic vent at the far end of the long attic that allowed some natural outside light to filter in. Tonight there would be none. He waited for his eyes to adjust while attempting to see what was there. Trunks, boxes, stacks of books, pictures, furniture, a rocking horse.

He was just about ready to take a few steps toward the light when he heard a shuffling noise over behind what looked like a stack of old furniture. Austin whispered aloud, "I don't believe in ghosts, so Hiram, if that's you, you can just go away because you're not real."

Austin held his breath. He may sound brave and convince himself that ghosts don't exist, but that didn't eliminate the possibility of ghosts being real. He was sure he heard something. Getting to the light didn't seem as important as coping with his own doubts and fears right now.

"I don't believe. You can't be real. You don't exist," Austin said while staring into the darkness.

"So, I'm just going to keep walking. You can come up behind me if you want, but I'm going to find my way out of here."

He kept walking very slowly, trying to see in the darkness where he was stepping to be sure it was safe. His progress was slow and his resolve was strong to find an exit from the attic without going out through the house downstairs. He was determined because he believed this was the way they could all be saved.

But the shuffling was catching up with him. With each step he took it continued. Austin had read about ghosts and knew that even if they existed they might be friendly and that sometimes ghosts were unsettled souls from their previous life. Now that could only matter if he believed in ghosts, and he didn't. It couldn't be a ghost in the attic, he kept telling himself.

And then he reasoned that Hiram had obviously liked children because he had carried a dollhouse and furniture down the steps for his kids, and if Hiram was there in the attic with him he should explain that he was trying to save the children and maybe Hiram would help him. So Austin started telling Hiram about what he was doing and why as he continued to walk.

Whether Hiram was really there or not, Austin felt like they had an understanding between them. He made it toward the end of the attic, which was better lit. To his right he saw a door that wasn't a full-size door but still would lead to somewhere. Now the shuffling stopped behind him and he went on alone, as if Hiram had served the purpose that was needed.

He stepped across the rafters, being sure each foot was secure before taking the next step. Falling between the rafters would be disastrous because he would fall through the ceiling into whatever was below. He reached the door finally and pulled inward on it while balancing himself. He felt a breeze. What he saw beyond the door amazed him. It was to the outside and led to a narrow catwalk on the edge of the house. He could see beyond the end of the catwalk to a roof that looked like it could lead closer to the ground below. He would just have to carefully get from here to that roof and to the ground to get away into the woods.

For now he needed to close this door and make his way back across the attic and back down the stairs and close the steps before Jo Lee missed him.

He very carefully stepped across the rafters to more solid footing straight down the middle of the attic to the steps and then felt for the pulley system, which would open the pull-down steps. Now, let's think about it. Would it work backwards to open the steps? It didn't seem to move and Austin experienced a moment of fear of being trapped in the attic unless he took a chance in broad daylight of using the catwalk and roofs to get away.

Let's be logical, Austin thought to himself. He couldn't be the first person to ever get stuck in this attic in the last hundred and sixty years. The steps must open from the attic.

He analyzed the pulley mechanism and pulled it in the opposite direction and ever so slowly the hole began to open and the steps dropped down. The only challenge to that was holding it back so that it didn't just drop with a loud bang. It burned his hands to hold it back. During this process he listened carefully to the sounds below to be sure Jo Lee wasn't yelling for him.

There, now he heard it at a distance and coming closer, "Austin! Austin, where are you?" Without a doubt it was Jo Lee. No one yelled like Jo Lee. Cameron's sick act must not have kept Jo Lee busy for long enough.

The steps were down and now he had to get down them and get the steps put back up before Jo Lee discovered where he was. He made it to the floor and pushed up on the bottom step to lift it up when he heard Jo Lee's voice even closer, "Austin, you'd better answer me!"

He got the steps up and left the rope hanging as it had been. Now he had to get out of this room before she caught him there and started to figure out he was up to something.

He heard her slamming doors as she went in and out of each room looking for him. He would have just a few seconds between slams to get out of this room and down the back stairs as she came closer to this end of the hall.

There was a slam. Okay. Now another door was opening, which meant she was going into another room. Now was his chance. He swiftly got out the door and quietly closed it behind him and ran around the corner and made it to the first step when Jo Lee yelled again, "Austin!"

Did she see him or was she just yelling again? He kept going down the steps taking two at a time in the midst of stares from the children below in the dining room. No adult was in sight. When he got to the bottom of the staircase, he passed through the dining room into the living room and heard Jo Lee yell again, "Austin, where are you? You'd better answer me now!"

With Cameron now asleep on the couch, with all the innocence he could muster, Austin yelled just loudly enough, "Jo Lee, I'm right here!"

"Where are you?" Jo Lee shouted from the top of the living room steps.

Again Austin responded sweetly, "I'm right here in the living room."

"Where have you been all this time while I was looking for you?"

"I've been trying to find you because I could hear you hollering for me, but I didn't know where you were. Now I found you."

Now at eye-level with him, Jo Lee looked right at Austin and said, "I don't believe you. Not for one minute. I don't know where you were, but you'd better watch your step because I'm right behind you, and I won't let you out of my sight."

With that innocent smile, Austin replied, "I'm so sorry I upset you, Jo Lee. I will try really hard to not make you angry again. Can I help you do something for dinner?"

Jo Lee wasn't fooled, but knew there was no reason to argue. Instead she answered, "Why, yes, Austin. How about peeling potatoes for dinner? That will keep you busy for a little while."

Austin said, "Sure, but I've never peeled potatoes, but I'm sure you would love to show me how."

CHAPTER 28

Austin spent the next three hours peeling potatoes while other children helped with laundry or read and played games. There was not the same excitement as the day before with the spelling bee. The children appeared to be growing bored with the limited activities.

Without the entertainment of their cell phones, computers, video games, and music devices the day seemed long. Some of the children wanted to go outside, but Jo Lee forbid that.

So, they were back to playing board games. Today there were longer, more intense ones like Monopoly, Life, and chess. Someone knew how to play Rummy and taught a few others. Parents would love to have this opportunity to play games with their children as a family. But there were no parents and no families. There were only children who were coping with a difficult situation, trying to believe they would get home, and parents who were frantic, afraid they would never see their children again.

The games got them through the afternoon. Stewart and Raole made an appearance, asking if anyone needed anything because they were going to the store.

Some of the children said they wanted cell phones and laptops and televisions, but no one had a serious need, so what they said was ignored. As they were turning to leave, one of the children said that Cameron needed medicine. The men looked to Jo Lee for approval. She shrugged and said, "Get him something for his stomach and aspirin. That should do it." With that they were gone. Marta and Jo Lee were left to watch the doors while keeping the children busy.

They waited until Stewart and Raole returned from the store before sitting down together to eat. Dinner seemed quieter than usual. The ham, mashed potatoes, and green beans seemed to satisfy everyone. Cameron ate everything on his tray, which was covered up by Austin, who grabbed Cameron's plate before Jo Lee could see it and wonder why he ate so well if he felt sick.

Homemade apple pie that Marta made seemed to lift their spirits. Ice cream helped even more.

The evening seemed long because the children had all helped wash the dishes and clean up after dinner, which really decreased the amount of time it took. Now they were all in the living room and dining room talking and continuing with games.

A particular conversation made Jo Lee uneasy as questions began to be directed toward her. "Jo Lee, do you have a job?" Melanie questioned.

Jo Lee was close enough to hear, but thought she could ignore the question. Not being around children much, she didn't realize how persistent they can be.

"Hey, Jo Lee," Melanie repeated the question louder. "Do you work anywhere?"

Now with every person in the dining room listening, Jo Lee felt it might be too obvious if she didn't answer. So, making up something seemed like a quick solution. "Yes, I have a job."

For Melanie and the others that was not a sufficient answer. This time Jessica persisted. "So, what is it?"

Jo Lee, caught up in creating a lie, replied, "I'm a flight attendant," which would be very unlikely, given the fact that Jo Lee did not like to be kind to people or take care of their needs. But, now that she had started the lies, one led to another.

"So, what airline do you work for?" Julianna asked.

"For many different ones."

"Wow, I didn't know you could do that. That would sure be a lot better than working for just one airline and going to the same places all the time. You could be like a substitute teacher and if you go to a school and don't like it, you just don't go there again. So you can just pick a different airline every week and see if you like the places you go." Celeste, ever the thinker, had actually contributed to Jo Lee's lie and made it more believable.

Jo Lee's response was, "Sure. That's what I do."

Stan heard this discussion and had his doubts about the truth of any of it, but decided it was certainly not worth arguing with Jo Lee about it. He only gave Zackary a look that said they were better off staying out of the conversation.

On the other hand, Jacob detected Jo Lee's slight uneasiness, and couldn't help himself from contributing to it. "So, Jo Lee, do you have a family that travels with you all the time?" Jacob asked.

"No, my family doesn't travel with me."

Jacob continued, "Oh, but you have a family?"

Now for more lies. "Of course I have a family."

Now Darius, otherwise fairly quiet since his spelling bee defeat, felt some interest in joining this conversation. "So, where is your family?"

Now Jo Lee felt like they were beginning to pry just way too much, and didn't like how personal the questions were becoming. "Okay. You can play some board games and then go to bed."

There were some groans, but Austin, who had been following the conversation, said, "Jo Lee, where's your husband live?"

Jo Lee had a glare with her eyes that she used when unhappy. Now she looked at Austin in a way that said, "You again," but said as kindly as ever, "Now, Austin, what game would you like to play?"

Max seemed to sense some tension, or maybe truly wanted to be a friend to Austin, said, "Austin, would you play Scrabble with me?"

Before Austin could answer, Nadialee said, "Yes, let's play Scrabble. And we can play over close to Cameron so that he can still lie on the couch and play, too."

Austin really didn't want to be bothered, but between now and tonight's escape he reasoned that the game would occupy his time.

"Okay. Who wants to play?" was Austin's answer. Way too many children volunteered to play Scrabble with him. Occasionally someone quietly arises to a leadership role without trying. This appeared to be happening with Austin. He certainly never intended to be a leader, and if asked, he probably would have said he didn't want to be. But it was almost as if the other children detected that Austin was up to something that just might help them all.

Jo Lee noticed the turn of events that seemed to make Austin a favorite among the children. Not understanding the minds of people, or even trying to understand how people think, let alone the reasoning of middle-school children, Jo Lee stored that information in her brain, but didn't stop to analyze the meaning of it. Later, possibly too late, she might realize the impact of Austin's ability to lead and think independently.

The Scrabble game began and the other children followed by choosing board games and card games, except for four of the 5th and 6th -grade girls, who decided to read a book aloud to each other. So, all seemed to be occupied for a little while and content with what light was created by the generator as it became darker within the mansion until Jo Lee announced that it was time for bed. Although it seemed forever to the children, tonight would be their third night since leaving North Middle School.

CHAPTER 29

Jo Lee followed the children up the steps, which gave Max a chance to help the cause without even realizing it. "Jo Lee, can't we have our flashlights back? It's dangerous walking around in the dark if we have to go to the restroom without any light. What if we fell down the steps?"

Ryan, followed immediately by Nadialee, begged Jo Lee to please give them back their flashlights. Some of the children were thinking about the ghost stories that had been told at breakfast, which added to their worry about having to be in the dark without flashlights. The thought of Hiram walking around in the hallway or hearing Emmeline's husband calling her name in the backyard could begin to instill some panic within the dark, scary house.

Stan said it was not fair to not give them flashlights. Jo Lee, not to be coerced by anyone, was going to argue, but Marta intervened.

"Let's just let them have flashlights. What's the worst that can happen? They have nowhere to go and no way to get there, so what harm is there in letting them have their flashlights?"

Jo Lee went into a spare bedroom and retrieved the flashlights, and handed them out. Not to give in too much too easily, she began to get her key out when they neared Zackary and Austin's room, now that Cameron was left with Stewart and Raole to sleep downstairs on a couch.

Now Zackary expressed his feelings, "Wait a minute! Surely you're not going to lock us in! What did we do? And do you really want to have to get up during the night when we have to go to the bathroom?"

Marta again intervened. "I think it will be fine to leave their door unlocked. They could even check on Cameron during the night so we won't have to."

Later Marta regretted again saying, "What's the worst that can happen?"

So, all the children were left in their rooms with flashlights and unlocked doors. "Now what were the chances that would happen?" Austin wondered. He was grateful that the others had fought the verbal battles to get them their flashlights and unlocked doors so that he didn't draw any attention to himself by Jo Lee.

They had just settled in their rooms when, as if on cue, Cameron could be heard from the living room crying out and moaning. The first scurry of concerned children appeared immediately at the top of the stairs looking down into the living room. Various comments were made by the children including, "He needs to go to a hospital, but Jo Lee won't take him because how would she explain who Cameron was and why she had him?"

"He needs to go home."

"We all need to go home."

Austin, hearing this, felt more motivated than ever to take care of things.

Jo Lee apparently heard the children from below, and yelled, "You kids get back to your rooms now!"

Now, while the adults were occupied, was Austin's chance. From the hallway he entered the room at the end of the hallway next to the boys' restroom while no one was looking and closed the door behind him. He was prepared with the flashlight to help him find the dangling rope, which he pulled immediately. This time he predicted the thud of the bottom step on the floor and prevented it from happening by using his hands as cushions between the bottom step and the floor.

He felt for the steps with his feet and ascended as quickly as possible. He knew now at the top where to find the pulley that would close the steps and hide the evidence of where he was. Now there was no turning back. This was just the beginning of Austin's true adventures.

He followed the same route he had earlier today to get to the other end of the attic. This time there was no shuffling. It was as though Hiram had served his purpose at last to help make children happy and so he didn't need to be a wandering soul any longer.

Slowly Austin made his way toward the far end of the attic, remembering to turn right where he thought the outside door had been. Now it was very important to be sure to stay balanced and have each foot solid before taking the next step. Falling between the attic rafters through a ceiling into a room below was not the way Austin wanted this adventure to end. It had been easier this afternoon to see the light from outside around the edges of the door he was looking for. Now there was only darkness outside that would not give him a hint of where the door was. Did it have a handle?

Austin couldn't remember because the light from the window at the end of the attic, and perhaps some help from Hiram, was all that he had needed to find the door. Now his flashlight was not helping to locate what he needed. It had to be here, thought Austin. I didn't imagine it. I even opened it, so I know it was real. I know there's a way out of here. Our only hope is for me to get out of here to the outside and go for help. I won't give up now. Besides, Jo Lee could already know he was gone, so he couldn't go back and face her anger with more excuses about where he had been when she already obviously had doubts after she had caught up with him this afternoon.

There in the eaves it looked like a glint of something shiny. It could be a door knob. He shined the flashlight again where he thought he saw something shining, and there it was. A crystal doorknob barely hanging on by a screw was there on the door. Now he had to carefully get there across the rafters without falling through.

As he pushed against the door and twisted the doorknob, it came off in his hand fortunately after the door became unlatched. He decided that putting it in his pocket was better than leaving it there for anyone who might follow behind him.

The cool air hitting his face showed that he had successfully found the outside. He closed the door behind him at the same time that he stepped away from it onto the catwalk. He hoped that the catwalk was still sturdy after many years of probably not being used. It felt solid, but was certainly narrow.

Austin had never had a reason to be concerned about heights. On the other hand, he had never been this high off the ground. He wasn't even sure in the dark how far below the ground was, but he did know that two floors below the attic of a house with really high ceilings meant that falling to the land below would be disastrous. He couldn't think about that. He needed to fully concentrate on staying balanced and keeping his feet moving to reach the end of the catwalk where it met the next roof that was thankfully closer to the ground. He could see the roof getting closer and was almost to the end of the catwalk. He wasn't sure what he would have to do next, but now the edge of the roof was only two steps away.

It appeared that to get to the ground below he would have to get on his belly and slide carefully to the edge to see where he needed to go next. Fairly quickly he was there. While holding onto the edge of the roof he felt with his feet and tried to see how close he was to something below that he could land on. It appeared that if he dropped just right he would be on a balcony. He quickly made a decision to try it. He landed on the rusted metal floor. From there he could see inside of the mansion into a room dimly lit by oil lamps. It was a space he had not seen from inside. He recognized clothes strewn across a bed and realized that those clothes were worn earlier today by Jo Lee. This must be her room and she had changed clothes recently. Did she plan to take Cameron to the hospital or did she change clothes to come looking for him?

He knew that if someone came out of the back of the house he would be visible where he was. He had no time to waste to get over the balcony and out of sight into the woods. There was a trellis against the wall that he reached with his foot when he threw his leg over the balcony. He hoped the trellis would hold and that the wood he was stepping on wasn't rotten. He hung onto the trellis with both hands as he stretched his legs down to find the next foothold for each of his feet as the ground got closer.

Finally he was on solid ground and he heard no voices. If anyone was coming out of the house they weren't close by. He could get to the woods from where he was in just a minute if he moved fast.

But what was that? It wasn't a voice he could identify. It was someone different yelling a name he didn't know. What did it sound like? A man's voice at a distance sounded like it was whispering, "Emmeline." There it was again. Now he remembered the ghost story. Was it possible? It was just too eerie to imagine that both ghost stories might be real.

He made a dash for the woods, hoping no one would see him. In less than a minute he was under the cover of the trees at the edge of the woods. In the breeze rustling the leaves, he kept hearing the voice softly calling, "Emmeline," but he didn't stop running until he was surrounded by bushes and trees and could no longer see lights from the mansion.

Since he had entered the woods from the back of the house, he knew the land was sloped downward. He had planned ahead to get down into the woods and go to his left because that was the direction Jo Lee and Marta had come from when they went to the store. He had paid attention to the direction the car was parked when they had helped carry in groceries. He decided that going to the left would take him to some civilization since that's the way they had come from shopping. Time would tell if his reasoning had been correct.

Austin had not anticipated how difficult it would be to walk through the woods at night even with a flashlight. It was difficult to shine the light ahead to know where to walk, but at the same time to still try to keep it shining at his feet so he could tell what he needed to step over. There were many leaves covering large rocks and roots above the ground, as well as low-hanging branches from trees. He felt like he was slowly moving along and not making any progress, but he was finally out of reach of the voice calling, "Emmeline," and no other voices or sounds could be heard.

He assumed, whether it had already happened or might happen during the night, that when Jo Lee found that he was gone, she would come after him or would send one or both of the men. At least they also would have to be on foot in the woods since there was no other way to get through it. His only option was to just keep going to try to find anyone who would believe his story.

CHAPTER 30

Jo Lee was not about to take Cameron to the hospital. She found a hot water bottle for him to put on his stomach. That should help whatever was wrong with him. He needed to just go to sleep, and when he woke up in the morning he would be fine.

With Marta's help, they got the children all back to their rooms. Zackary knew better than to tell anyone that Austin seemed to have disappeared. Although they had not discussed anything, he had suspected that Austin was planning something because of how devious he had acted and how he had questioned Jo Lee about everything. Now he wasn't there and, although curious, Zackary stayed quiet to see what happened next. The pillows piled under Austin's covers had fooled him temporarily. Maybe that would trick Jo Lee also.

Zackary didn't know how long he had been sleeping when he awoke to a voice and a light shining in his face. "Zackary," Marta asked. "Where's Austin?"

"What? Austin? He's over in his bed. Why?"

"Jo Lee sent me up to check on him."

"Well, he's right there asleep."

"Okay. Go back to sleep."

Hours later, as it was beginning to get light outside, he was awakened again, but this time by Raole yelling. "Jo Lee, Austin isn't here! His covers were pulled up over pillows. When was the last time you saw him?"

Jo Lee came in with her face red and her hands shaking as she uncovered the pillows further. "Zackary, where is he? You have to know where he is!"

"No, I don't. I had no idea he wasn't over there in bed."

"When was the last time you saw him?"

"I don't know. It was dark and we got up when we heard Cameron. I didn't look to see if Austin was here and I didn't talk to him. So I don't know."

Now giving orders to Raole, Jo Lee told him to get Stewart to search the house to see if they could find Austin. "And, Zackary, don't try anything funny. I'm not sure I believe you. You and Austin have been a problem since the beginning."

Zackary said, "I didn't do anything."

Jo Lee glared at him before she left the room while saying, "Make sure you don't. When we find Austin we'll get to the truth. You'd better have your story straight by then."

Then she turned and gave orders to Raole on her way out the door, "You and Marta need to find him. If he's not here, then get the van out and start driving. He's on foot, so he can't be far. Stewart! Go look in the woods. Austin's gone!"

CHAPTER 31

Austin had been walking for hours, just hoping his theory had been right about which direction to go. So far, there had been no signs of life other than forest animals – deer, rabbits, squirrels, raccoons, skunks, owls. He knew these woods also contained coyotes, bobcats, foxes, and black bears. But fortunately he had not encountered any of these during the night.

Light from the sun rising was beginning to penetrate the dark woods and shine down through the leaves. Now would begin an even more dangerous time for being spotted by anyone looking for him, which he assumed by now was probably happening.

If he could just make it to a road, he could follow it and find someone who would help him, but so far there had been only woods. He had heard no sounds except for the crunching of his own feet walking on acorns and dried leaves. But now he thought he could hear the traffic moving somewhere at a distance and water flowing close by. He walked toward the sounds of the water since he knew that creeks often flow next to roads, thinking that the water would lead him to where the traffic would be.

Austin's reasoning was correct, but he was not able to predict how quickly someone from the house could be where he was by car on the very road that he thought might save him. He knew what the van looked like, but couldn't believe that one of the first vehicles that he saw from his hiding place beside the road was that van. He was so close that he saw Raole and Marta, but thankfully they couldn't see him behind the rock and in the bushes even if they had looked in his direction.

Well, at least he knew that more than likely they were searching for him, and he knew where they were even if they didn't know where he was. Since he was on the side of the road, he would just keep following it in the same direction that Raole and Marta were going because it probably led to the town. Staying in the bushes would keep them from seeing him if they came back this direction.

The sun was fully up when Austin started to see what looked like the beginning of a town. Surely there would be someone who would help him. His story would sound so pathetic that they would have to believe him. No one could make up a story like this.

Not seeing the van, Austin thought he was safe marching into the police station and getting the first person to help him. What he had not counted on was Raole and Marta arriving before him with a story of their own.

So, when he approached the policeman sitting at the front desk and began telling him about the kidnapping, he got stopped abruptly. "They said you might come here with this made-up story about kidnapping. Don't you realize how much your parents care about you and want you back? They were just in here and told us how worried sick they were last night when you got mad and ran away from home. They left their phone number that I'm supposed to call if you showed up here. So I'll just give them a call."

"No! " Austin wasn't sure that it was his voice screaming, but the days of frustration and hours of trying to reach help were catching up with him.

"You've got to believe me! Don't you watch the news? It's bound to be on the television. Twenty of us were kidnapped from North Middle School the other day and we were brought here to a mansion. I ran away last night to get help. Don't call them! You've got to help the others get away."

Apparently Austin was loud enough that Sargent Denise Fazio heard him from the next office and came to check out the situation. She asked the officer at the desk what was going on, and he explained Raole and Marta's visit and Austin's story.

Before she could respond, Austin said to her, "You've got to believe me. I've been kidnapped."

Austin being so convincing made her realize that something needed done about the situation. "I believe you, but let's go talk to my boss. Meantime," turning toward the front desk, "there'll be no phone calls made yet."

Then, turning toward Austin, she said, "Do you want some hot chocolate?"

Above the door was a sign that read Captain Duncan. The captain was in his office and willingly listened as Austin drained his hot chocolate and told his tale, even at times nodding his head as if completely understanding. He left twice during the story - once to get a fax to hand to Denise. Next, he left to get the phone number for Raole and Marta from the front desk.

Seeing the paper with the phone number made Austin feel like crying for the first time since the morning they left school. "Please don't call them. There's a lady there named Jo Lee who will start hurting the kids if she knows I'm here."

"Austin. Your name is Austin, right? Calm down. I can't imagine surviving what you've been through, but you have survived, and that's what's important. Not only did you survive, but you have gotten the help your friends need to get them safely home. I needed the phone number to make a different phone call – to the FBI. Within a short time they will be able to use this phone number from Raole and Marta to locate where the children are and get them out safely. Although we don't have much local cable access, we stay informed through faxes and Internet about what's happening nationally. You've been all over the news. Now I need to make that phone call. Finish your hot chocolate and Sargent Fazio will show you the restroom. You're safe here."

CHAPTER 32

When Raole and Marta arrived back at the mansion empty-handed, Jo Lee was furious. Even worse than them not having Austin was that they had given Raole's cell phone number to the police.

"What were you thinking? Didn't you think that this story might just be on national news? If someone there puts it altogether, we're sitting ducks just waiting here for someone to find us. In fact, we need to get out of here and we'll leave your cell phone here, which will lead them here – but we'll be gone. Okay. Gather the kids and get them in the van. We've got to get out of here fast!"

CHAPTER 33

Even Jo Lee was not faster or smarter than the FBI or the local police. Within minutes of Captain Duncan's phone call, the FBI was mobilized into action with information from the local police officers, who were joined by the State Police until the FBI arrived.

Although the cell phone was left in the house, the local police knew where the abandoned mansion was and the road that led to it. It took them only minutes to gather forces with the State Police and be on the road racing toward what they hoped was a positive outcome.

The van was traveling away from the police, however. Assuming that if the police were looking for them they would be coming from the direction of the town, they would go the opposite direction of the town to try to outrun them. They would have probably been successful except that the FBI uses helicopters. They were able to track the van filled with nineteen children and four adults. If not done carefully, there was a risk of losing everyone in the van over a hill off one of the winding roads without guardrails.

The helicopter pilot knew the van's location and was able to land where the road intersected a major four-lane route. With the police behind them and the FBI in front of them, Jo Lee and the gang didn't have a chance.

When the van stopped and the FBI ordered everyone out of it, Stewart threw the van in reverse to go back the way they came, but the police cars arrived behind them blocking his way. Now police officers and FBI agents were out on foot surrounding the van from which no one had exited.

Now van doors were opening and Stewart and Marta stepped out first with their hands raised. Next, Jo Lee opened a door and got out, but had to be told twice to put her hands up. Only Raole remained in the van with the children and the same duffle bag from the last bus ride. Were there explosives?

As Raole finally exited the van he reached into the duffle bag instead of raising his hands, and in that one second of him not paying attention, an FBI agent ran from behind the van and jumped on Raole, throwing him to the ground. Raole's hands were put in handcuffs while another agent grabbed the duffle bag. There were no explosives or fire arms in it – only his hat, a toothbrush, and some newspapers.

Were there explosives still in the van with the children? They hadn't emerged from the van. There was only one way to find out. One agent got into a seat in the van and asked how the children were and if they knew if there was anything dangerous in the van. They all said that Raole had it in his duffle bag. It seemed that the scare tactic had worked not only for the children, but also with Principal Rollins. No explosives even existed.

CHAPTER 34

The six o'clock news that night reported the capture of four kidnappers. Not to go down by themselves, they gave the law enforcement the information they needed to take into custody the men behind the operation that had involved the threat to the children and the blackmail attempt of five million dollars.

Not only the capture of all involved was reported, but the safe return of all twenty children to their families was discussed, along with the bravery of the children, especially one named Austin, whom it was agreed had risked his own life to save the others.

There would be an assembly to celebrate all of the children's safe return and to honor Austin and those students like Cameron, who was definitely a good actor, and Zackary, who stood up for what was right when it was necessary. Students who had been in school together, but had not really known each other, had now formed a bond for life.

Their lives would never be the same after this experience. Never again would they take for granted the things in life like family and home and safe schools – and they all had a greater appreciation for the value and capabilities of technology in their lives.

Absent from the assembly would be Principal Mark Rollins. Although not directly involved with the circumstances leading to the threat or the blackmail attempt, he had definitely used unwise judgment that could have led to twenty children being harmed. The School Board voted to replace him. He would be able to spend time now becoming familiar with his personal finances and his home. There would be a hearing to determine the extent of Liz Rollins' involvement with providing information that made the job too easy for the blackmailers to arrange the kidnapping.

Video-footage on national news showed the parents hugging their children and a camouflaged bus being towed out of the bushes and trees. It was reported that this bus would be recycled to serve a different purpose.

The Last Bus: Time Matters

ABOUT THE AUTHORS

Debbie and Greg are thrilled to be the parents of seven children and, at this time, eight grandchildren. Proud to be Mountaineers, several of their degrees, including their doctorates, have been earned at West Virginia University. Both have been educators for many years and are currently university instructors and principals; Debbie of a middle school and Greg of a high school. Many hours for writing together are provided when commuting to work and traveling to visit family. The Last Bus was selected in 2012 as a Finalist in the National Book of the Year Contest sponsored by the National Association of Elementary School Principals.

The Last Bus: Time Matters

Made in the USA
Charleston, SC
17 October 2013